Every Month Original Novels, Stories, and Articles

Smith's MONTHLY

USA Today Bestselling Writer
Dean Wesley Smith

TABLE OF CONTENTS

SHORT STORIES

FULL NOVEL

SERIAL NOVEL

NONFICTION

SMITH'S MONTHLY ISSUE #35

Introduction
THREE SHIPS AND A DREAM

Back in October of 2015, in *Smith's Monthly #25*, I published a Seeders Universe novel called *Star Mist*.

That novel introduced three major Seeder ships engaged in fighting a war and how the six chairmen got in charge of the three major ships.

Star Mist was one ship and the focus of the first book, *Star Rain* was the second ship and the focus of the second novel, and *Star Fall* was the third ship.

The two novels in *Smith's Monthly #25* and *#26* told the story of the big war. And that all wrapped up in those two books.

But *Star Fall* still had a story to tell. And that's the novel that is in this book now almost a year later.

You do not have to have read the previous two novels in this mini-series inside the Seeders Universe to read this book. There are a lot of years between the end of *Star Rain* and the start of *Star Fall*.

But this novel takes the Seeders Universe and expands it even more, which seemed impossible.

But it does.

And the next book in the series after *Star Fall* will be called *Starburst*. You'll understand as you read the prolog of the novel in this issue. And that will make even more sense when you get to the end of the novel.

I have always wanted to write a massive science fiction series set in space covering distances so vast as to be flat impossible to imagine. I imagined worlds like these since I read Doc Smith's Lensmen series and his Skylark series as a kid. Now I am doing just that and I am having a blast writing these.

When I wrote for *Star Trek*, many people told me I should write that kind of science fiction in my own work. Back then I felt almost afraid to try it because of my admiration for such massive science fiction universes already in existence.

But somehow I managed to get the Seeders Universe started, sort of like

Thanks for the Support

Dean Wesley Smith

3

how Doc Smith started the Skylark series, actually.

And now *Star Trek* is a tiny little universe compared to the Seeders Universe. But yet I feel the same feeling from *Star Trek* and Doc Smith's novels comes across in these Seeders novels.

Or at least I hope it does.

I also hope you enjoy the story of the third major ship in the Seeders Universe Star series. I am very proud of these books.

And this universe I have created.

Sometimes childhood dreams do come true.

—Dean Wesley Smith
Lincoln City, Oregon
August 12, 2016

The Seeders Universe Novels
Now Available from all your favorite booksellers in trade paper and electronic editions.

Coming Next Issue in *Smith's Monthly*
LAYING THE MUSIC TO REST

Smith's MONTHLY

NUMBER THIRTY-SIX
SEPTEMBER, 2016

*Original Stories,
Novels, and Articles*

DEAN WESLEY SMITH

LAYING THE MUSIC TO REST
My First Published Novel

USA TODAY BESTSELLING AUTHOR

DEAN WESLEY SMITH

SHE TURNED HER BACK
ON DEATH AND PICKED
LIVING FOREVER

THE CAVERN
A THUNDER MOUNTAIN STORY

Stout used to own the Garden Lounge where the time-traveling jukebox sat. He sold the Garden to live with his love, Jenny.

Now Jenny's cancer diagnosis gives her only five months to live.

Bonnie and Duster, the original owners of the jukebox, will not stand for that diagnosis.

A Thunder Mountain story of love and death and living?

THE CAVERN
A Thunder Mountain Story

ONE

RICHARD CONE SAT at the kitchen counter in the huge underground cavern below the Historical Research Institute.

Outside, the summer heat had hit close to one hundred, but the cavern was cool and comfortable.

Dawn Edwards had just fixed herself and Bonnie Kendal some soup and a ham sandwich for lunch when Richard had come wandering in. He looked like he had lost something and even though Dawn didn't know Richard very well, she had always seen him with a smile on his face.

Not today. He looked every bit of seventy years old and he walked like an old man instead of the spry bartender who owned the Garden Lounge, a small local bar on the outskirts of Boise.

She had offered to make him some lunch and he had nodded and thanked her, then sat down at the counter.

Bonnie looked at Dawn with a raised eyebrow. Something was very, very wrong.

Around them the huge cavern was empty except for the three of them at the kitchen area counter.

The cavern was mostly a central location for all alternate time travelers, with living room furniture in various groups in front of a huge fireplace, a long kitchen counter, a giant kitchen large enough for five people to work behind the counter, and large restrooms and showers tucked off to one side.

Travelers using the Institute time travel sort of gathered in this area when not either in their apartments sleeping, doing research or writing in their offices, or back in time for a short trip.

In 2025, since there were so few time travelers, the room got very little traffic and was way overbuilt, but hundreds of years in the future Dawn knew this room had people in it all the time.

Actually, Richard was from a hundred years in the future and would need to return and reset at some point, since he was aging so much. He had been living in this timeline for over forty years now, but in 2120, when he was from, he will have only aged two minutes and fifteen seconds.

That allowed all time travelers to live thousands of years.

Richard had come back to this time period on the request of Bonnie and Duster to help out with an experiment in music penetrating time. They had built a jukebox to test theories on sound cutting through time and Richard had put the jukebox into the Garden Lounge, owned by a wonderful and kind man by the name of Radley Stout.

And Richard had then spent years being a regular customer in the bar, monitoring the use of the jukebox.

Dawn really, really liked Stout and his wife, Jenny. Two of the nicest people on the planet.

Richard now owned the Garden Lounge after buying it from Stout and loved it. Every Christmas Eve a bunch of them from the Institute went in to have drinks with the wonderful regulars there who knew about time travel but really didn't know about the Institute or seem to care.

And every year they toasted the jukebox and all the lives it saved, even though it no longer worked. No one but Stout and Jenny and Richard knew the jukebox that could take people back to their memories had been removed and replaced by a duplicate that was just a regular machine.

But everyone who was a Christmas Eve regular had been affected by the time travel aspects of the original jukebox, so they all toasted it every year in memory.

Stout and Jenny knew about the Institute and Richard. They had traced the jukebox back to here when it stopped working five years earlier. But they were not travelers, even though at one point Bonnie and Duster had offered to have them travel back in time.

They both had said they were very happy right where they were at. They had all their friends at the Garden Lounge here in Boise and her family with her first husband in the Bay Area.

Richard and Stout and Jenny seldom stopped by the Institute or the big cavern. In fact, in the last two years, Dawn couldn't remember even hearing that they had come to the Institute.

And now Richard showed up, looking very down and sad.

And alone.

Dawn put the chicken soup and ham sandwich in front of him, then took her plate from beside Bonnie and moved it to the back counter so she could see Richard and Bonnie and it would be easier to talk.

"So," she said, "what's happened?"

Richard just shook his head. "Jenny's got cancer."

"Shit," Bonnie said. "How bad?"

"Bad," Richard said. "They just found out yesterday and told me today."

Dawn felt like she had been punched. Death and dying of those they got to know in the past was a normal course of events. It never made it easier. Never.

Richard shook his head and stared at his food. Then he said, "I've lived almost four thousand years in various timelines and I would trade all of that to keep Jenny alive."

Dawn knew the feeling exactly.

TWO

DAWN WATCHED AS Bonnie shook her head, took out her cell phone, and walked away as she hit a number.

She headed across the big cavern with a purposeful stride. Bonnie clearly had some idea. All of them felt like they owed Stout for taking such good and respectful care of the jukebox experiment. But Dawn had no idea at all what Bonnie was thinking. More than likely, she was calling her husband, Duster, to tell him.

"So how is Stout taking this?" Dawn asked Richard.

"Typical Stout," Richard said. "Calm and collected on the outside, ripped apart on the inside. The two of them only had five years together."

"Damn," Dawn said. "That's not a lot of time."

"Too damn short," Richard said, picking at his sandwich and then deciding to work on the soup first.

At that moment, Bonnie turned and started back toward them. She had walked over toward the fireplace and clearly was now done with her call. That hadn't taken long at all.

Bonnie walked right up to Richard. "Get Stout and Jenny in here now. This afternoon. And don't take no for an answer."

Richard started to open his mouth, a puzzled look on his face.

"No questions," Bonnie said. "Just go get them and get back here."

In all the years of being around Bonnie, Dawn had never heard her speak like that.

And since she and Duster were the two people who controlled the Institute and everything about it, Richard just nodded.

He pushed his plate forward and stood.

"I'll save it for you," Dawn said.

"Thanks," he said.

Then when Richard got out of hearing going toward the elevator that led up to the Institute main mansion above them, Bonnie turned to Dawn. "Where is Madison?"

Dawn looked at her funny. Why did she need Dawn's husband? What in the world was going on?

"He's up north working on some research," Dawn said.

Bonnie nodded. "Duster will call him and get him on board, then. But call him first and tell him about Jenny and to expect a call from Duster in a little bit."

Bonnie sat down at the counter and went back to work on her food.

Dawn called Madison, told him what had happened and told him she had no idea what was happening.

"He'll be waiting for Duster's call," Dawn said to Bonnie when she was finished.

Bonnie nodded.

"So you want to tell me what you are thinking?" Dawn asked as she wrapped up Richard's sandwich and put it in the fridge.

"We're going to break some major Institute policies," Bonnie said. "And I need all four of us on board, as well as Jesse."

Jesse was the Institute director. There were fourteen original founders of the Institute, the first fourteen that Bonnie and Duster had taken back into the past. So basically on most things, the fourteen ran everything, had board meetings, and so on.

And they had all set up the Institute policies at the start. Those policies supposedly were lasting for hundreds of years into the future so far.

But since she and Madison had been the first two that Bonnie and Duster had taken back, and Jesse was the director, if the five of them decided something, it was decided.

Dawn was about to ask Bonnie exactly what the policies she planned on breaking were, then it occurred to her what Bonnie was thinking.

"We're going to take Stout and Jenny into the future, to cure her, aren't we?"

Bonnie nodded. "In 2220, cancer is pretty much something that is easy to fix."

Of all the people in this timeline, only Bonnie and Duster had gone that far forward. Dawn and Madison had only gone a hundred years into the future, riding with two from the Institute at 2120 who had come back to get them.

Sometimes Dawn forgot that her life actually was anchored a hundred years in the future. And if something happened to her or Madison here, today, they would have only spent a little over two minutes in the future. But they spent so many thousands of years in the past from here, she never remembered the fact that only two minutes for her were really passing.

Basically, everyone who used the Institute was immortal for all intents and purposes.

"You on board with the idea?" Bonnie asked.

Dawn looked at her friend, someone she had known now for thousands of years.

"One hundred percent on board," Dawn said. "Not sure how you are going to pull it off, but I'm on board."

Bonnie nodded. "That's three of us then," she said. "Duster likes the idea."

Dawn nodded. If Duster and Bonnie were both on board, then this was going to happen.

She just hoped the repercussions wouldn't tear things apart.

THREE

STOUT AND JENNY sat at the empty bar in the Garden Lounge. They were holding hands and it felt right to be here, as far as Stout was concerned. The dozen booths, the chairs for all the regulars at the long wooden bar, the faint smell of cleaning solution and whisky. This was his home, his safety.

It didn't make Jenny's cancer diagnosis any better, but sitting in their normal places at the bar seemed to make them both feel better for the moment.

Richard had said he would be late and they could just go in without him.

They had just come from the doctor again this morning, a second opinion, and there was no doubt that Jenny had stage four cancer. They were giving her six months, tops. Nothing anyone could do.

Outside the heat of the day was baking but the air-conditioning of the bar was holding it back, making everything comfortable.

"We're going to need to tell the kids," Jenny said, holding her glass of orange juice over ice that he had poured her, but not drinking it.

Stout smiled at her, took one of her hands and squeezed it. She was always the practical thinking one. And she had taken this news almost in stride after a short session of crying as he held her.

She was not the type to feel sorry for herself, but instead just face forward to the future. Even as short as it was now looking to be.

Stout couldn't even imagine the coming Christmas Eve here in the Garden without her sitting beside him as she was doing now.

This morning, the second doctor confirming her diagnosis had only seemed to firm up her resolve and spirit.

He had no idea what he was going to do without her. He just couldn't let himself think about that. Right now she was here, sitting beside him, and he was going to treasure every moment they had together from this point forward.

He almost couldn't remember all the decades before the last five years that he had lived without her. Those no longer seemed real.

"We'll figure out a way to tell them," Stout said.

"Since their father was taken by cancer," she said, "this is going to hit them really hard. We're going to have to help them."

Stout shook his head and turned and smiled at her.

"You raised three of the strongest humans I have ever had the pleasure to meet," Stout said. "They are going to help you, not the other way around."

She laughed, squeezing his hand back. "Yeah, I suppose so."

At that moment Richard unlocked the front door and strode in, letting it bang closed behind him. He strode up to them.

"I have been ordered," he said, "to take you both to the Institute as quickly as possible."

"You told them?" Stout asked, surprised.

Richard nodded. "I just needed someone to talk to and since you two are my best friends, talking with you seemed out of the question. So let's go."

Stout just shook his head. "I can't see what they can do to help."

"Yes," Jenny said. "We're fine. But thank them."

Richard laughed. "Seriously? They are the ones that built that jukebox time machine, remember? The one that helped you two get together. Duster has more knowledge in his little finger than I have learned in thousands of years of living. And there are more advanced degrees in that building than in a hundred universities combined."

Stout jerked at that. He kept forgetting that Richard was from a hundred years in the future and had lived at least three or four thousand years in different timelines in the past before he bought the Garden in this timeline.

To Stout, Richard was just Richard, his best friend and the only person he would have trusted with the Garden Lounge and a time travel jukebox.

Jenny glanced at Stout. "They might be able to help. It won't hurt to find out."

Stout nodded and stood. "Got any idea what they are thinking?"

"Not a clue," Richard said. "I told Bonnie about your cancer. She seemed to get angry and went off, made a phone call, and then came back and ordered me to come and get you. Bonnie and Duster started that place and they never order anyone around, so I jumped."

"Clearly Bonnie has some sort of idea," Jenny said, shaking her head. "I really like her."

Stout did as well. He liked all the people from the Institute that he had met. And he always enjoyed having them join them for Christmas Eve here in the Garden. But he wasn't going to let any hope creep in after this morning.

He just didn't dare.

FOUR

DAWN WATCHED AS Richard led Stout and Jenny toward the large kitchen counter across the cavern, moving through the couches and chairs and coffee tables. Both Stout and Jenny looked healthy and trim and in great shape. Much better than Richard had looked when he came in this morning.

Of course, Stout and Jenny were both younger than Richard by at least twenty years in this timeline. If she remembered right, both of them were just in their late 50s.

Bonnie stood and gave Jenny a hug.

Dawn went around the counter and also gave Jenny a hug.

Dawn really liked Jenny and Stout. Two wonderful people all the way to their cores.

Then, after talking for a moment, Dawn went back and got out Richard's sandwich and slid it to him. Then asked Stout and Jenny if she could get them anything to eat or drink as they settled in at the bar.

"Look at this," she said, "me an amateur serving two professional bartenders."

"Eventually we'll get you trained for the big time," Stout said, smiling and Jenny laughed.

"I would be honored to learn from the masters," Dawn said.

She then got both Stout and Jenny some orange juice over ice as they requested.

"So what's this all about?" Richard asked.

"We're going to fix Jenny's cancer," Duster said from behind them.

Dawn glanced up as Duster and Jesse came into the large room from a side entrance.

Jesse was the only one of the founders who was as big as Duster, and strode step-by-step with Duster toward the kitchen area. Both of them had on short-sleeved shirts and jeans and tennis shoes.

Jesse came over and shook first Jenny's hand, then Stout's hand as Duster introduced Jesse as the director of the Institute. Clearly they had not met before,

but Dawn knew that Jesse had followed closely all the work on the jukebox and how Stout had carefully handled the jukebox for years.

Duster and Jesse both went around behind the large counter beside Dawn so that they could face Richard, Stout, Jenny, and Bonnie.

"How are you going to fix Jenny's cancer?" Stout asked.

"Actually," Duster said, "we're going to cure it."

"That's not what the doctors have said is possible," Stout said.

"And they are correct," Jesse said, looking at Jenny. "Here in 2025. The type of cancer you have is incurable."

Jenny frowned. "How do you know what kind of cancer I have? We haven't told anyone, not even Richard."

Duster raised his hand. "I needed to get your exact medical records," he said. "So there might be a new cancer treatment and research center being added onto the hospital over the next number of years in your name."

Dawn laughed. Typical of Duster. Just typical.

Bonnie laughed also, looking at her husband. "You bribed them to give you her records?"

"A large donation," Duster said. "But it was important to have the records and I am sorry I had to do that, Jenny," Duster said, turning to her. "I hope you will forgive me once we get you all fixed up."

Jenny laughed. "Not sure if I should be angry or honored, so I'm deciding to go with honored. Thank you. But I could have gotten them for you for a lot less."

Duster shrugged. "The hospital needed a new cancer research center. And I promise, no one but me and Jesse

will ever see the records and they will be destroyed when this is all finished."

Dawn laughed. All of them had more money than they knew what to do with in hundreds of corporations. She had a hunch the money Duster donated didn't even make him blink.

Jenny and Stout both nodded.

"So what is the plan?" Richard asked.

"The plan first off," Jesse said, "is for not a one of us to ever talk about what we are about to do to anyone outside this group."

Dawn laughed. "Breaks a few Institute policies, huh?"

"A few," Jesse said, nodding. "But this is something we planned for, to be honest."

Duster and Bonnie nodded.

"We have a special hidden area for possible cases just like this," Bonnie said.

Now that surprised Dawn more than she wanted to admit, since she and Madison had been with them since almost the beginning and had helped them plan and build this Institute. Every detail, she thought.

Seems, they kept a few details from her.

And not for a second did that surprise her.

FIVE

STOUT JUST FELT shocked about the very idea that Jenny could be cured of the cancer. He hadn't been willing to accept the diagnosis at first, now he was having trouble accepting a possible solution.

But Jenny seemed to be fine with it. She was treating this like just another thing to deal with caused by the sickness.

For a moment the silence in the huge cavern just felt heavy.

Finally Jenny asked, "So what is exactly going to happen?"

"We're going to jump you directly two hundred years into the future," Jesse said. "We have two people jumping back from that time who will be your guides. Duster and I and Bonnie will meet you there."

At that point in time," Bonnie said, "two hundred years in the future, we have a medical facility here in the Institute that has been doing advanced research on all sorts of various human illnesses."

"Your type of cancer was cured just over a hundred years from now," Duster said. "So two hundred years in the future, the cure for your cancer is common and fairly easy on you."

"That sounds wonderful," Jenny said, smiling. "I like easy."

Stout squeezed her hand. This sounded too good to be true, but when it came to Jenny living more than a few more months, that's what they needed.

"How long will we be gone?" Stout asked.

"About thirty minutes from here," Duster said. "But you will need to spend a few days in the future."

Stout started to open his mouth to ask a question and then shut it. Over the years he had dealt with all sorts of puzzles about time travel. That wasn't the focus at the moment. The focus was getting Jenny well.

"Now," Jesse said, moving a step closer to Jenny and Stout and putting his hands on the counter in front of them, "there are a few repercussions, problems if you will, of this action that may sound silly to you at the moment, but they are deadly serious and I want you to consider them before agreeing to this."

Stout nodded. "Here comes the too-good-to-be-true other shoe."

"In a manner of speaking," Jesse said, "yes."

Stout glanced at both Duster and then down the bar at Bonnie. They were both looking very serious. Dawn and Richard just seemed to be as confused as he was.

"Go ahead," Jenny said.

"First off," Jesse said, "by taking this treatment, there is a side effect that can't be helped. The treatment is going to also slow down your aging. You will look about ten years younger, you will feel younger, and you will live for at least another hundred years, if not more."

Stout stared at Jesse for any sign of a smile, but clearly Jesse thought this was very serious.

"That's a side effect?" Jenny asked.

"It is," Jesse said. "And I have no idea if either of you have any moral or ethical or religious objections to that."

Stout couldn't help it. He actually laughed.

"I can look and feel a decade younger?" Jenny asked. "Be cured of the cancer and live for a few hundred more years?"

"Exactly," Jesse said. "But realize that you will age slower than your children by a long ways. At some point you will have to stage your deaths and then watch them from a distance only."

"Oh," Jenny said.

Stout was starting to understand as well. What a horrid decision. Her children either watch her die in a few months or she lives long enough to watch them die.

"What is the second problem?" Stout asked.

Jesse nodded to Duster to tell him.

"If we jump you two hundred years in the future," Duster said, "and then you come back about thirty minutes after you leave, you will, for all intents and purposes, be immortal."

"Like I am and everyone else is here," Richard said, nodding.

Stout looked at the much older face of his friend. Richard had once told him that when he returned to his normal time he would be young again.

"How does that work exactly?" Jenny asked before Stout could.

"Because of the nature of all this," Bonnie said, jumping in, "once you are in the future, that is now your natural time. So when you come back here, you can live for hundreds of years and then die and when you die, you will find yourself back in the future just slightly over two minutes after you left, at the age and physical well-being of the moment you left."

"Then you can turn around and come back to a point in the past again," Duster said, "and live more lifetimes."

"You can do that as often as you like," Richard said. "That's why I have lived thousands of years, yet in my own time, I have aged very, very little. In fact, in my time, I only joined the Institute about six months before."

Stout looked at Jenny, who seemed to be a little shocked at all this. But he was understanding everything pretty clearly, thanks to a few conversations with Richard.

"Here is what they are saying," Stout said, turning to face his beautiful wife. "You can be cured, we both will feel a decade younger and healthier, and we will live a long time. In other words, instead of only a few months together, we can spend lifetimes together, if you want."

She looked at him, then did something he never expected Jenny to do. She burst into tears and hugged him.

After a moment she pulled back slightly. "You want to spend lifetimes with me?"

He brushed some of her tears away off her soft cheeks. "If they can figure out a way to make it longer than hundreds of lifetimes," he said, "I would take that as well."

She smiled. "Damn you are good, Mr. Radley Stout." Then she kissed him.

Then she wiped off her eyes and turned to Duster, then to Bonnie, then Jesse. "Thank you for your wonderful offer. If you don't mind too much and it doesn't cause too many issues with the Institute, I would like to accept it, side effects and all."

All Stout could do was hug her as around them the others cheered, filling the mostly empty cavern with the wonderful sound of applause.

Then he pulled back and looked down the counter at his smiling friend, Richard. "This next Christmas Eve," he said, "that old jukebox really needs more than one toast of appreciation. It will have saved yet another life."

"You're both going to be there to give them," Richard said, smiling. "That's all that matters."

To Stout, Richard was right. He and Jenny would be there.

Together.

And that really was all that mattered.

USA *Today* Bestselling Writer

DEAN WESLEY SMITH

THE LADY OF WHISPERING VALLEY

A Buckey the Space Pirate Story

Buckey's best friend loves to recite limericks and can travel in time. Not bad for an oak tree named Fred.

But Fred must help Buckey and the love of his life find a way to live together. Not an easy problem considering Mary lives a hundred years in the past.

But an oak tree that recites limericks knows tricks of time.

Can true love be blocked by the simple passing of time?

And can Fred come up with a limerick that fits the situation in time?

THE LADY OF WHISPERING VALLEY
A Buckey the Space Pirate Story

ONE

"WHY IS IT that I don't see you in your space pirate costume anymore?" Fred asked, his voice filling the air around me but seeming to come from no one location.

I tried to ignore him and focus on my textbook for advanced economics for a final I had coming in a week.

Fred was my talking oak tree friend. I had planted him in my mother's backyard a number of years back as an acorn. He now stood almost twenty feet tall. I spent a lot of time studying in a lawn chair under his shade in the summer, considering I was in my last year of college to get a degree in business with a combined major in horticulture. Having a talking oak tree for a best friend could get a person interested in growing trees and other plants.

I knew it was kind of sad that a talking oak tree, who had a fondness for limericks, was my best friend, but it was true.

Pathetic, but true.

Fred could not only talk, but like all oak trees, he could travel through time to where other oak trees were in the past. And if I was holding onto him, he could take me along as well, a trick that had come in fantastically helpful for a couple history classes I had been taking.

Six months earlier, he had taken me into the past and introduced me to a wonderful woman my age named Mary that he talked to as well. She lived in 1871 outside of Boise, Idaho.

We had fallen for each other instantly, as Fred knew we would.

Mary was my age of twenty-five and had been widowed three years earlier. She lived alone in a cabin surrounded by oak trees. She had wonderful brown hair that mostly she kept pulled back and large brown eyes. I was five-ten and she was five-five and we made the perfect couple, or at least Fred told us we did. I tended to agree with him on that point.

I spent a lot of time in her cabin with her. She was the love of my life, even though as far as I was concerned, she had been dead for almost a hundred and fifty years.

We were working on that problem, or we both wanted to, but mostly we just didn't talk about it. Living a few miles apart or a city apart might have been something we could fix, but living over a hundred and forty years apart seemed to be far too much.

So we just enjoyed the time we had together, thanks to Fred, and ignored the big problem.

Besides meeting and falling in love with Mary, what was nice about Fred being able to take me there was that he could bring me back to within seconds of when I left, even though I had spent a week or more with Mary. That kept me from missing too many things in this time.

And he could return me after a week in my time to within an hour of the last time I left Mary.

"Well?" Fred asked, not letting go of his question even though I ignored him the first time. "Why don't you dress like a pirate anymore?"

I closed the book and sighed. "Honestly, I dressed in my Buckey the Space Pirate costume to go to science fiction conventions to meet girls."

I had to admit, it was a good costume. Tights tucked into tall black boots, a long coat with brass buttons, a wide belt with a sword hanging from it at a suggestive angle, and a wide-brimmed hat with a big feather.

Girls loved it.

"I have gotten a little old for that now," I said to Fred, "and besides, if you have forgotten, I have a girlfriend now."

"Oh, yes, I do remember our first meeting with you in your costume," Fred said. "Something about a punt and a runt and..."

"Don't even go there," I said, remembering that date I had with a wonderful woman with a body that would never end. She and I ended up down in the park under Fred, before he was cut down and before I saved him by planting him in my mother's backyard.

Fred had decided, right at the wrong moment, as my date and I had a meeting of the bodies, to spout some limerick about the size of a certain part of her body.

She had thought it me insulting her and had never talked to me again.

Considering what Fred had said about her body part in that limerick, I didn't blame her in the slightest.

"As I said," trying to stop him talking about that night, "I have a girlfriend now."

"Well," Fred said, "not actually now in the literal sense of the word, but I understand your meaning."

"Thank you," I said. "I sure wish Mary could spend time here with me. It would make things so much easier."

"She can," Fred said.

With that, I damn near fell off my lawn chair.

TWO

AFTER I REGAINED my balance, I looked up into the leaves of the little oak tree. "Why didn't you tell us?"

"Neither of you asked," Fred said. "You seemed very comfortable in the situation in Mary's cabin."

"How?" I asked. "How can she come here?"

"The same way you return to her time," Fred said. "If she was here she would need to stay over oak roots or under oak limbs to remain. Same rules you follow in the past."

"Would you mind bringing her here?"

I thought I could hear him laugh slightly. Fred often laughed at me. After standing around and thinking for hundreds of thousands of years, it seemed oak trees had a superiority complex.

A moment later Mary was standing with her hand against the young oak tree, looking around.

I again damn near tipped over my lawn chair again as I rushed to stand up and hug her.

"Do not move too far," Fred said. "My young roots have not expanded out to even a respectable length yet."

Mary felt wonderful in my arms.

She had on her riding jeans and a light blouse and a wide-brimmed hat. More than likely Fred had suggested she prepare for a warm summer day.

After I kissed her, she looked around, smiling. "So this is where the young Fred of your time resides."

"This and in every other oak tree on the planet," Fred said, sounding a little indignant. He did that a lot.

Mary laughed and kept staring at her surroundings.

I glanced around at my mother's backyard, seeing it for the first time in a while. The yard had a chain-link fence around it and a small shed to hold the lawnmower to one side, but otherwise it was just a patch of mowed grass with a small and snide oak tree growing to one side.

And mom's house looked like any other house along the street from the back, with a small covered back porch and a couple chairs on it.

I just hoped mom didn't take this moment to look out the window. If she did, I was going to have some explaining to do.

I pointed out to Mary what few landmarks there were in the backyard and then said to Fred, "Could you jump us downtown near where you and I met. The street there is lined with oak and Mary can get an idea of what the modern world is really like."

"That is a splendid idea," Fred said.

A moment later Mary and I were standing under a massive old oak in a large park in the center of the city.

Traffic sped past on the two-lane road that bordered the park and some thirty- and forty-story buildings towered nearby.

She took my hand and grasped it tightly. I couldn't even begin to imagine what she was feeling.

"Oh, my," Mary said, staring first at the cars and then at the tall modern buildings, "the future is a wonder-filled place."

"That it is," I said.

After a moment, she turned to face me, a look of worry in her eyes. "What do you see in a simple woman from the past like me?"

For some reason I had my wits about me at that moment. "I would love you no matter what time you came from. But do you love me because I live in this madhouse of a time?"

"Of course," she said, kissing me. Her smile when she pulled away could light up a room.

And I think I was smiling just as large and wide.

Suddenly, being born almost a hundred and fifty years apart from the woman you loved didn't seem like such an insurmountable problem.

THREE

AFTER WALKING ALONG the park for a ways, staying under the large oaks, I finally turned to Mary. "I love you. If you are willing, I would much like to start talking about how we solve this living situation we find ourselves in."

"Why Mr. Buckey Pirate sir," she said, smiling at me. "Are you asking me to live in sin with you?"

"I am, my fair lady," I said, bowing slightly and pretending to tip my hat. "And a wonderful sin it will be."

"Then how can I refuse such a sordid offer," she said, smiling, "if we can figure out how to work out this confusion of two worlds."

"I may have a few suggestions on the living aspects," Fred said, his voice almost echoing under the large oaks. "Not in the matter of the sin aspect. However, if needed, I have watched many thousands of human couples in copulation over the centuries and I am sure that..."

"Fred," I said, holding up my hand. "Thank you."

Mary was blushing and laughing.

"Could we go to Mary's cabin and the three of us have a discussion?" I asked.

Mary nodded. "Yes, please."

A moment later we were standing inside Mary's wonderful log cabin tucked into a stand of oaks in 1871 in a narrow valley outside of Boise, Idaho. The valley was called *Whispering Valley* for a reason I had not yet asked Mary about.

I really loved this place with its wonderful river-stone fireplace and large overstuffed furniture, including a couch that could lull anyone into a nap.

And Mary had a featherbed in her bedroom like nothing I could have ever imagined sleeping on. Why modern mattresses had gone to firm and hard was beyond me. Mary's featherbed just almost wrapped around me and cradled me to sleep.

Of course, having Mary beside me didn't hurt that feeling of contentment.

When we arrived, the large main room of the cabin smelled of fresh bread and light wood smoke, a combined smell that I knew I could never get tired of.

Mary made us both a cup of tea from the hot water she had left on the wood-burning stove before she left to visit me. I actually, in her time, had only left her about three hours before. But in my time I had attended a few classes, spent a night in my apartment studying, and taken one test.

We sat at her kitchen table, facing each other. I told her what I had done over the last day since I had left earlier this morning.

She nodded and said, "I can now, after this short excursion into your time, finally start to visualize some of what you talk about. I hope to learn much more about your time."

"I hope you can live there with me as well, as I live here with you," I said. "Fred, is that possible?"

"Very much so," Fred said, his deep voice filling the kitchen and living area as it always did.

"I worry," Mary said. "Are we not to become a burden on you with our constant requests to move back and forth through time?"

I nodded. I worried the same thing.

Fred chuckled. "I have lived for hundreds of thousands of years. My species, which will include me, will live for a hundred thousand years into the future. I will far outlive you both and will treasure our short time together and write limericks about you both for many to enjoy into the future."

I laughed. "So that means you won't mind?"

"It will find it no bother at all," Fred said.

Mary looked at me and smiled. Then she said to Fred, "If I haven't said this lately, I would like to say this again. Thank you for introducing me to this fine man."

"You are more than welcome," Fred said.

I could almost imagine Fred bowing to Mary. If an oak tree outside of a Disney cartoon could bow.

"So what is your suggestion?" I asked Fred.

"You must learn to think as a person unstuck in time," Fred said. "I know humans have no sense of time and very little memory. So this thinking will be a strain, but I can help."

Mary frowned. She had no idea what he was talking about either.

More Buckey the Space Pirate Stories
Available at your favorite booksellers.

"Would you try that idea again with a few fewer insults to humanity and a few more concrete ideas?" I asked.

"Create your home here, in this valley, to live in at any point in time," Fred said.

Suddenly I realized what Fred was driving at in his usual Fred fashion.

"Do you own this home?" I asked Mary.

She nodded. "And the one hundred and eighty acres around it as well going up the valley and on both sides of the valley. My husband's father homesteaded it and passed it on to his son and I got the land and the home when he died."

I could see in Mary's eyes that she was starting to understand as well.

"You will need to plant a lot of oak trees all over this land in the coming years," I said to her.

She smiled. "That will be my pleasure."

"And mine as well," Fred said.

"And I need to do some research on how to pass this land down in trust," I said. "So that I will inherit it at the age of 25."

"That sounds like a very logical solution," Fred said.

I could hear in Fred's voice the sound of almost pity at the poor stupid humans. And it dawned on me why.

"Of course, in my time," I said, "Mary has already set up the trust and the land is about to transfer to my name. Is that correct?"

Fred chuckled. A condescending chuckle, but I'll take it.

"Can we see what we will work so hard in this time to accomplish in a future time?" Mary asked.

"Of course," Fred said.

A moment later they were standing near the remains of her old cabin, long since crumbled to a pile of rotted logs. I could see the stones of the fireplace to one side. Weeds covered the remains.

"Now that makes me sad," Mary said.

"We can build brand new," I said.

She nodded and turned to look around.

A forest of tall, strong oak seemed to spread over the landscape and down a shallow hill and around a stream.

As far as they could see under the canopy of oak, the land remained clear and empty.

"You left forty acres unplanted down on the lower side to sell off to get money to build a dream home here," Fred said.

"Wow," Mary said, looking around. "I planted all of these? This is wonderfully beautiful."

"You both will plant these," Fred said, his voice echoing again in the shady, cool area of the old oaks.

"How will I be able to move beyond the roots of leaves of an already planted tree?" I asked.

"Look to your right about ten steps," Fred said.

We followed his instructions, but all we could see were acorns littering the ground.

I picked one up. "Is this what you are talking about?"

"It is," Fred said. "You hold in your hand the essence of the beginning of life of my species."

I couldn't believe what I was thinking.

"Are you telling me that if I carry around an acorn in Mary's time, and she carries around one in my time, we can go anywhere?"

"Of course you can," Fred said. "As long as you do not remove the acorn from your person outside of the influence of an oak tree's branches or roots. If you do, you will just return to your own time where you left."

I glanced at Mary who was looking shocked as well.

"Why didn't you tell us?" I asked.

"You did not ask," Fred said. "It is one of the great failings of all humanity, actually, to not ask the right question at the right time. I have watched the results of that for far longer than I care to remember."

"But you can remember thousands of couples copulating," Mary asked, smiling at me.

"That is a very different matter," Fred said. "And fodder for many a limerick, I might add."

"I can only imagine," I said.

"No need to imagine," Fred said. "I would be glad to share as many limericks as you would like to hear about the copulation patterns of your species. For example:

"There was a young woman from Spain,
"Whose body seemed quite plain, ..."

"Fred," I said, interrupting him, "I promise to listen to your limericks but right now I think Mary and I need to get busy making sure this wonderful place comes to pass. We have a lot of work and planning to do."

"I agree," Fred said.

"And we need to get on with this planning to live in the sin offer I have been made," Mary said, smiling at me.

I pretended to tip my hat. "That my lady, will be no work at all. Only pleasure."

She kissed me and I kissed her back.

We stood there under the large oaks in the beautiful valley, holding and kissing each other until Fred said simply…

There was a young lady named Grace,
Who loved to be held in embrace.
She hugged and she tugged
But no lover remained
For her lips were on the side of her face.

I'm fairly certain Mary laughed first, even though we both knew that laughing at the oak tree's limericks did nothing but encourage him.

~

Can't Get Enough of Poker Boy?
These stories and more are available at your favorite booksellers.

USA TODAY BESTSELLING AUTHOR

DEAN WESLEY SMITH

LAYING THE MUSIC TO REST

A former college professor turned bartender, Doc finds himself trying to save his friends from a ghost under a lake in the wilderness of Idaho.

From diving into a ghost town buried under a lake to trying to stay alive on the sinking deck of the Titanic, *this time-travel science fiction novel reads like a roller-coaster ride with all the twists and turns.*

First published in paperback in 1989 from Warner Questar Books, Dean Wesley Smith's first published novel gives a lot of hints of his future series and his bestselling career spanning over a hundred and fifty novels.

Published here in its original form, without any changes, just as Dean wrote it almost thirty years ago.

LAYING THE MUSIC TO REST
Part 8

CHAPTER FOURTEEN

Boat Deck
Fourth Cycle
April 14, 1912

THE BITE OF the wind against my face and the weight of the pack on my back felt absolutely wonderful as the blackness faded and, for the fourth time, was replaced with the orange and reds of an Atlantic sunset. I took a deep breath of the salty-tasting air, quickly lowered the pack to the deck, and headed at the quickest run I could manage for the doors to the grand staircase.

I was going to try to beat that guard woman to stateroom C-85.

We all were. That was our plan. We had spent the last two hours of the cycle in the first-class lounge, drinking and discussing exactly what we should do next. The first hour we had sat in the same booth. But as the tilt of the ship became more pronounced, Marjorie and I could no longer hold ourselves on the stern side of the seat. We had to move to the bow seat of the nearest booth and then turn around to talk down to Alex and Craig. That kept me continually reminded that I was on a sinking ship.

Outside the windows the passengers scrambled in all directions. I tried not to watch, yet found my gaze drawn to the deck. I kept having a sudden desire to run out on the deck and work at building something that would keep me afloat. But the totally unconcerned nature of my three companions kept me inside. It certainly didn't help my nerves any that during the entire last hour we could hear the clear ragtime tunes of the band from the deck above. I must have had at least six drinks to try to keep from shaking. I hoped I was going to get used to this real soon. Or find a way home.

We ended up not having enough information to form any concrete plan of action or even an educated opinion as to what was actually going on. Everyone had seen the woman standing in front of the stateroom. And everyone had gotten the same impression I had. She was guarding the door and she was not someone to be taken lightly. Susan might or might not be in that stateroom. The controls to the mirror might or might not be in there. The woman might or might not be an enemy. We just didn't know.

So the one conclusion we came to was that we needed more information. We assumed that the woman had gotten here the same way the rest of us had and therefore was governed by the same cycles we were. She too would have to come from outside that circular perimeter and return to the stateroom at the beginning of each cycle. It might

be possible to beat her there. Maybe see if there was anyone else in that room.

So, the plan was simple. All of us would rush as fast as we could from our cycle locations and then calmly walk through the stateroom area. None of us were to do anything other than act like prisoners passing through. If there was no one around, someone could take a quick peek inside the room. Alex was going to stay in his original clothes and act like a regular passenger. We'd all meet back in the library as soon as we could afterward.

Running at my fastest, I made it to the A-deck landing without being too winded. At the landing above B deck, where stained-glass panels framed the staircase, I almost bumped into a woman and a small child passenger. By the time I reached the landing above C deck, I was gasping for air. It seemed that five years in a smoke-filled bar had cut down my strength and lung power.

Alex was climbing the stairs from D deck two at a time as I reached the lush C-deck foyer. "You go right," I managed to tell him between breaths. "I'll take the left hall."

"Careful," he said as he jogged past me and through the port-side door. I didn't have the wind to answer him. He was seventy years older than I was. How come I was the one breathing hard?

I paused for two quick breaths to give my heart a chance to catch up, then crossed the wide checkered-tile foyer. I had to wait for two passengers to pass before I could open the door to the starboard hallway. I was about to start down the long, carpeted stretch when I heard Susan's voice behind me.

"You're not going to be able to keep this up," Susan said, her voice nasty and filled with anger. "Not for long. My people will get through and then we'll deal with all of you."

I turned around. Susan was being escorted up the grand staircase by two others. The guard woman was on Susan's right, and a man wearing similar brown slacks and a white shirt was on Susan's left. He looked to be no more than five foot ten, with huge swimmer's shoulders and chiseled facial features. Susan's hands were tied behind her back. She seemed to be offering no physical resistance as she was led along.

As they turned the corner off the stairs and headed across the foyer toward the door I was holding open, Susan saw me. She seemed to almost pause in mid-stride, but not quite. Amazing control. The only acknowledgment she gave me was a slight shake of her head.

I understood. With one quick look into the man's intense gray eyes, I started down the hall letting the door close behind me. I figured I had about five seconds before they got to that door and got it open. No way could I make the almost two hundred feet to the center corridor in time without looking suspicious. But I could do my best to put some distance between us.

I did my best imitation of a sprinter down the wide hall and past one woman passenger headed in the other direction, counting to five as I ran. Marjorie, dressed in a blue bathrobe, was striding toward me. She was almost at the center cross-corridor.

"They're right behind me," I shouted at her, trying to keep my voice just loud enough for her to hear. She stopped, a frightened look on her face.

"Warn Alex if he's in the hall, then go the other way." She nodded and turned off the main hall into the middle corridor.

I reached my five-count and slowed to a walk as I heard the door from the foyer of the grand staircase open behind me. Susan was no longer talking. I was amazed she had even said what I over-heard. If I were her, I'd be afraid they'd dump me overboard.

I tried my damnedest to look like I was just another prisoner ambling along, bored, while doing everything I could do to get some sort of air into my poor lungs. As I reached the center corridor, I could see Alex and Marjorie heading for the port-side hallway. Craig was standing at the other end waiting for them. I didn't make even the slightest motion at them, but instead walked right on past the corridor and then did everything in my power not to look back until Susan and her two captors had turned off toward C-85.

The moment I figured they were around the corner, I waited another two counts and then nonchalantly glanced back. No one in sight. I went back and peeked around the corner. I was in time to see the guard woman press some sort of small, calculator-looking device against the door. She made a twisting motion with the calculator and the door swung open. All three went inside and shut the door.

Alex, acting nonchalant, walked slowly past the other end of the corridor. I was about to signal him that I would meet them back upstairs in the lounge when I caught a glimpse of something.

A tall, very thin man was coming down the starboard hall behind me from the same direction Marjorie had come. This guy was wearing the same type of brown pants with a light brown, long-sleeved shirt. He also had a very wide brown belt around his hip with a gun strapped to it. He looked like a walking skeleton, so tall that if the hall light fixtures had been on the ceiling instead of the walls, he would have had to duck around them.

If I was ever going to have a heart attack, that would have been the moment. I had no idea if he had seen me peeking around the corner, or the start of my signal to Alex. I didn't know whether to run for it down the center corridor past C-85, head back toward the grand staircase, or walk right at him as if nothing at all was out of the ordinary. I knew right off I couldn't handle any more running for a few minutes, and the thought of walking right at this giant was more than my heart could take. So I took the easiest way. Without looking like I was running, or even in a hurry, I headed back the way I had come, any moment expecting to hear the loud thumps of his footsteps as he overtook me.

Somehow I covered the two hundred feet of nightmarish hall and made the door. As I went out into the foyer of the grand staircase I took my first look back.

He was nowhere to be seen.

*

Alex and Craig were already in the first-class lounge when I came through the door. Craig was standing beside the bar and Alex was fixing drinks, dodging around the regular bartender like it was a child's game. He still wore his 1909 suit and looked extremely out of place behind the *Titanic's* bar.

I waved at them and headed for the booth, weaving my way in and out of the cloth chairs and intricately carved tables. I needed to sit down. I'd had to make one stop climbing the two flights back up to the lounge and I still felt winded. On top of that I had enough adrenaline pumping through my body to last through a week of horror movies.

As I dropped down into the booth, Marjorie came through the back entrance

of the lounge. She was still barefoot, but she'd changed from her bathrobe into a pair of men's slacks and a white button-down blouse. She said something I couldn't hear to Craig and then both of them headed for the booth.

"You all right?" she asked as she slid in beside me and touched my arm. Craig sat down across the table.

"I look that bad, huh? Just a little out of breath is all. Not used to running stairs."

"Who is?" Craig said. I noticed he was breathing a little harder than normal, also.

"Here we are," Alex said, setting four glasses down on the table and then sliding in beside Craig. He placed a double scotch in front of me. "Thought you might need that."

"Thanks," I said. "After that last guy, I sure do."

"He gave me quite a turn," Alex said, laughing to himself.

"What last guy?" Craig asked. "What happened? After you yelled, Marjorie and I didn't dare look back down the corridor."

"Just a second." I took a good solid drink of the scotch and let the flavor roll around my mouth and the slight burning in my throat help clear my head. It was amazing how drinks taste better when you are in stressful situations. It was as if every sense suddenly came out of a dark room into bright sunlight. After a second quick drink, I set the glass down and held it between my hands. It tasted too good to let get away.

"They have Susan," I said. "A man and the guard woman hauled her up the grand staircase. She saw me, but I assume she figures I'm alone. They did something to unlock C-85 and then took her inside. About thirty seconds later this skeleton-like giant came down the starboard hall. He was wearing some type of revolver. I didn't notice guns on the other two. I don't know what happened to the skeleton guy. I didn't want to look back."

"He went inside," Alex said. "After a moment the woman came back out and is now standing guard again."

"Anyone got any ideas?" I asked as I took another drink. I didn't. And I hoped if anyone did, it would be a while. I desperately wanted to rest and sip on a few more drinks.

After all, there were two more full hours until this damn ship started sinking again.

CHAPTER FIFTEEN

Boat Deck
Fourth Cycle
April 14, 1912

WITH COLD FINGERS and while walking as fast as I could toward the entrance to the grand staircase, I clicked the last cartridge into Fred's rifle. I yanked the bolt back hard to pull a shell up into the chamber, then closed the bolt and made sure the safety was on. I was still ten feet away from the double doors.

"Nicely done," Alex said. "Would you like to try one more time?"

I shook my head and handed the rifle to him. "I can do it."

But I didn't like it. All I really wanted to do was get in out of the cold.

After an hour of talking in the lounge, we had formed a plan. We would again try to beat the Lomax, assuming that was who was holding Susan, to room C-85. Using Fred's rifle and a crewman's pistol,

we would surprise them at the corner of the starboard hall and the central corridor. With a little luck, we would free Susan.

Simple really, only no way in hell was I going to go pointing a gun at anyone. Not that I didn't know how. The Navy had taught me how to do it in boot camp. Somehow, I had been lucky enough to get through that. I had never fired a shot since. I even hated the thought of hunting. But Craig and Alex didn't seem to have the same trouble. Therefore, the plan was that I was to load the rifle on my way down, then give the rifle to Alex in front of the grand staircase on C deck. He would do any pointing that was necessary.

I had practiced digging the bullets out of the pack and loading the rifle on the run three times. After my first practice loading, Alex had blown some pretty good-sized holes in a row of wooden deck chairs. He said he wanted to get used to how the gun handled. I felt ready. Alex said he was ready. I just didn't like what we were doing.

As far as I was concerned, we didn't have enough information to go attacking anyone. I wanted to wait and continue to watch. But both Craig and Alex had argued that there was a large chance that they might kill Susan and that the sooner we acted, the better chance she would have. Besides, they said, there wouldn't be any shooting. We would surprise them and do it without a shot.

I argued that if the Lomax hadn't killed Susan yet, they weren't going to. That had sounded lame the minute I had said it. Yet I could think of no reason why they hadn't killed her. Nor could Craig or Alex. And the big question was how they kept capturing her every cycle. It made no sense. Of course, that was nothing new on the *Titanic*.

Alex laid the rifle down on the pack and we headed inside. No matter how many times I walked up and down that staircase, I would never get used to its incredible beauty. The oak rail and wrought-iron balustrades, the carved wood panels on the walls, the carved stone statues at every turn, the glass dome over it all. It made me want to stop and stare.

At the first landing I glanced up at the wall clock. I suddenly remembered the name of that famous clock. "Honor and Glory Crowing Time." It read 11:30. Ten minutes until the ship hit the iceberg. Two hours and forty minutes until the next cycle. A long time and not damn long enough.

Craig and Marjorie stood at the end of the bar, talking and sipping drinks. Craig had gone down to see how long it would take him to get to the crewman's gun. Marjorie had walked C deck to see if anything had changed. I glanced around the lounge. Except for two waiters, the bartender, and two passengers, the lounge was empty and felt cold.

"Any trouble?" Craig asked as we worked our way across the luxurious room, around the empty tables toward them.

"None," Alex said. "Doc had no problem finding the shells and loading the rifle. We shouldn't be slowed down by more than a few seconds over last time."

Craig nodded. "Good. I will take maybe ten seconds longer, but I think I can make up a few of those seconds by coming up the stern first-class stairway instead of the second-class stairway. It might even turn out to be slightly faster."

I went around Marjorie and behind the bar to fix myself a drink. If this kept up, I was going to start enjoying drinking again.

"Alex?" I indicated the well.

"Yes. Thank you," he said.

"Any change?" I asked Marjorie.

"Not that I could tell. The guard is still in the same place." Marjorie looked down into her brandy and swirled the golden liquid around and around in her glass. "I had a thought. If we capture these people, what are we going to do with them next cycle?

They'd be prepared for us a second time. And if they keep capturing Susan every time, won't they do it again next time?"

I nodded and so did Craig. The same question had crossed my mind. I hoped Susan would have the answer. I didn't want to face what we might have to do if she didn't. I supposed a ship that size had a lot of hiding places.

"We'll decide that after we see what's inside that room," Craig said. "Everyone agree?"

No one said a word.

Craig nodded. "All right, let's find a seat and make sure we've got this plan straight."

We were halfway to the booth when a faint rumbling shook the tables and lightly tinkled the crystal glasses behind the bar. My stomach again clamped up like I'd been hit with a solid right. My three friends didn't even seem to notice, but I was getting damn tired of this ship sinking.

An hour and a half later I talked Marjorie into going with me up on the boat deck to listen to the last few songs of the band. For some reason, it made me feel better to be out in the open, even though I refrained from madly wrapping deck chairs together.

For three songs, we stood, arm in arm, leaning against the rail, listening to the fantastic music of those brave men. Marjorie felt solid and warm against my side. I wished we had the time to sit and talk and laugh and learn about each other. But we didn't, so we didn't talk. We just stood and leaned against each other and listened. Considering what we were about to try, listening to the band on the *Titanic* seemed somehow very appropriate.

*

My fifth sunset didn't look anywhere near as good to me as the first four. This time my hands were shaking so badly,

I almost couldn't get the pack off. I dropped two shells and it took me until the landing above A deck to get the rifle loaded. From there, to make up for being late, I took the rest of the stairs two at a time all the way down. I reached C deck completely winded, panting, and with my heart pounding like it was trying to hammer out a rock tune on a set of drums.

Alex bounded up the stairs before I even had a chance to slow to a walk. I handed him the rifle and the box of shells as we crossed. He was going to go down the port-side hall and then be in the central corridor when the Lomax holding Susan came around the corner. I was to be near the central corridor and walk back past them so I would be behind them. Craig was to come from the stern along the starboard corridor. That way we'd have them completely surrounded if they came up the same way as last cycle. A good-sized if. All bets were off if they didn't.

Marjorie was to stay over in the port hallway and stand watch in case they came up that way. Or in case we weren't successful. If we weren't, she was to go and tell other prisoners what had happened and try to enlist their aid. That was Craig's idea. I didn't really want to think about what not being successful would possibly mean.

"Loaded?" Alex asked. He didn't even seem out of breath.

"Safety's on," I managed to gasp out. "Be careful."

"You too," he said.

Twenty seconds later I was leaning against the wall at the intersection of the center corridor and the starboard hall, desperately trying to get some air into my lungs. Without warning the door from the grand staircase opened and the two Lomax with Susan between them came through.

Alex was in place in the center corridor, Fred's rifle ready. Craig would reach the ambush corner at exactly the right time. Acting as nonchalant as the lack of air in my lungs would let me, I ambled down the hall directly at them, keeping my gaze locked on the carpet and the line where it met the oak panels on the right side of the hall. I kept telling myself I wasn't frightened. And I kept not believing it.

I met Susan's group halfway between the door and the central hallway. I moved against the right wall to let them pass and I purposefully avoided looking at Susan, but did glance up and catch the guard woman's glance. She nodded a slight hello and I found myself nodding back, as if we were simply meeting on a park sidewalk.

The moment they were past me, I stopped and pretended to be checking a cabin door on the left of the hall. At the moment I figured they would be reaching the corner, I turned around and headed toward them. Damned if I knew what I was going to do to help, especially against guns, but I figured I might as well be close.

As the two Lomax and Susan started to turn the corner, I heard Alex shout "Halt!" Craig, who was within a dozen feet of them in the main hallway, pulled his gun out of the back of his pants, dropped into a combat firing stance, and pointed it at the guard woman.

Everything froze, as if someone had turned the world down to ultraslow motion. Nothing more would have happened if everyone had stayed put as Alex had ordered. That was the plan and for an instant it seemed it was going to work.

But we didn't count on Susan.

Without warning, she shoved the guard woman hard with her elbow, then tried to yank away from the other Lomax. The guard woman hit the side wall, rolled toward Craig, and came up with a gun in her hand. Craig never stood a chance. Her low, muffled shot opened a wide gash across his chest. He jerked backward against a door and dropped with a hard thud to the carpet.

A moment later, a deafening explosion filled the hall as Alex fired Fred's deer rifle. The Lomax who had been struggling with Susan spun twice and smashed hard into the wall, then crumpled. He was facing me and I could see the life leave his body as his open, shocked eyes clouded and became frozen in a death stare.

The high-powered rifle bullet had passed through the Lomax and slammed Susan backward. Her head cracked hard against the oak paneling and she slumped to the carpet. Blood pumped from the large hole in her stomach, soaking her blouse and pants.

"Don't!" the guard woman shouted in very clear, very understandable English. She was lying on the carpet in firing position, her gun pointing down the central corridor at Alex. I couldn't see Alex, but I doubted if he had had time to pull another shell up into the chamber of the rifle. I also knew she would not hesitate in killing him if he tried.

"Drop the rifle!" Her command didn't allow room for argument.

I heard a dull thump as Alex dropped the rifle to the carpet.

"Back up," the woman ordered Alex. Then she glanced my way. I had taken a half-dozen steps toward the fight and then stopped. "Come down here." She motioned with her gun where she wanted me to be as she slowly got to her feet.

I moved down the hall toward the bloodstained carpet and wall. Alex's shot had sent both Susan and the man spinning and their blood had covered the walls and carpet like a splatter painting at the fair. I had to walk right through the middle of that painting.

A large, brown stain was forming under Craig's body. From the way his body lay, twisted unnaturally, he too was obviously dead.

It was everything I could do not to gag. The huge lunch Constance had fed me wanted to climb back up my throat. The copper smell of the blood mixed with the thick odor of gunpowder made me dizzy. I forced my attention on keeping the contents of my stomach in place as I neared the corridor intersection. Somehow I made it through the blood but I felt numb. My hands were tingling.

The guard woman backed up enough to let me into the central corridor. Alex was standing there, his face completely drained of color, his hands in the air. He was staring at the bodies of Susan and the man he had killed.

The rifle was lying off to the right side of the corridor. I went and stood beside him and she motioned for us to move on toward C-85. We hadn't taken more than a few steps when the tall skeleton man came around the corner from the port hallway pushing Marjorie in front of him. He held a small gun in his right hand and looked upset.

Marjorie was still in her bathrobe and seemed unhurt. Her eyes were wide with fear. As she got closer, she looked past us to the bodies and the blood-covered walls. For a moment I thought she was going to do what I almost had done. I could see her choking, fighting to regain control. Finally, she closed her eyes and let out a deep, shuddering sigh. I moved forward to support her, but she was holding her own. I put my arm around her shoulder and her arm went around my waist. I wasn't sure who was holding up whom.

"What happened?" the skeleton man demanded of the guard woman.

"They attacked us. Lawrence is dead," she said. "The Lomax is dead. I hit one of their members. He is around the corner to the right." She motioned back down the hall without taking her eyes off of us.

"Craig?" Marjorie asked. Her weight against my arm suddenly got heavier.

I hugged her arm and could feel her shudder as she tried to hold together. In all the last few hours of planning, we had not considered it could possibly turn out like this. I had felt there was a chance someone might get hurt or killed, but when I thought that, I didn't have a full realization of what it meant. It's one thing to see death all the time inside a nineteen-inch box sitting in your living room. It is quite another to smell the blood and feel the responsibility as a person dies.

I didn't want to watch, but I made myself as the skeleton man went down the hall and checked out first his own named Lawrence, then Susan, and then finally out of sight down the hall to look at Craig.

It was as we were standing there waiting that what the guard woman had said finally sunk through the fog in my mind. She had called Susan a Lomax. I had been assuming they were the Lomax.

The skeleton man came back around the corner and held his gun on the three of us until the guard woman got the door open and then stepped back, holding her gun trained evenly on us. It was very clear she was a soldier. She didn't seem the slightest bit shaken that she had lost one of her own and killed another man. One cold woman.

"Inside," the skeleton man ordered, his voice unable to hide a tone of disgust.

Alex led the way, followed by Marjorie and then by me. The room looked very much like Alex's room down on E deck. There was a built-in couch and bed, one padded chair, a small table, and a dresser.

"Search them," he said to the guard woman, "then take care of the bodies before they are discovered."

While he held his gun steady on us, she patted us down like an expert, not missing an inch, then took short pieces of twine and tied our hands. She made mine painfully tight. So tight that I knew there was no way I could pull out. I hoped blood could get to my hands.

She pointed to the couch. I sat on the left side nearest the door. Marjorie was in the middle and Alex against the wall.

As soon as the guard woman had gone out the door, the man sat down on the bed across from the couch and looked at us. "Who are you?" he asked. His voice sounded tired, as if he was facing a task he didn't want to face. "You first." He pointed at Alex.

Alex shook himself and then took a deep breath. "Alex Meredith, formerly of Boston."

"And you?" He pointed at Marjorie.

"Marjorie Thiel. I'm from Flagstaff, Arizona."

The man's eyes took on a shocked look of surprise which he quickly tried to mask. "And you?" He pointed at me. Now his tone was different.

"Kellogg Jones. Boise."

This time he made no effort to conceal his surprise. He shook his head and muttered a soft "Damn."

I wasn't real sure I liked the fact that my name was causing a stir. It had done the same with Susan and I had no idea what it meant. I had a feeling it wasn't good.

The skeleton man got to his feet and paced back and forth in the limited space. Up close, he looked even more like a skeleton. He was unbelievably thin and tall. His skin was pure white and his clothes hung loosely on him.

"I'm afraid to ask this," he said after a few moments of pacing, "but who was your friend?" He made a slight gesture toward the hall.

I looked over at Marjorie. I had never known Craig's last name.

"Craig Kendall," she said. "I'm not sure where he was from. I never heard him say."

For some reason, the tall man looked relieved. He went out into the hall, pulling the door closed behind him.

"Are you both all right?" I asked.

Marjorie nodded. "I think so. What happened?"

"Alex and Craig surprised them as we planned, but Susan spoiled things by jumping in the middle of it. The woman shot Craig and Alex hit their guy. The bullet went through him and hit Susan."

There was a long silence in the room. I went back over the disaster in the hall. How could we have been so stupid as to think surprising them would work? We had jumped into a situation that we knew nothing about and now Craig was dead. And Susan was dead. My one hope of getting back. I pushed that thought away and turned to Marjorie. "How'd you get caught?"

She shook her head. "I was so stupid. When I heard the shots, I glanced around the corner. I saw she had Alex and was motioning for you also, so I turned and started to run. He was coming in the stern door. He just pointed his gun at me. I guess he heard the shots and figured I was in on it. If I would have not panicked and walked…or gone the other way…"

"Don't worry about it," I said. "This entire thing was a mistake. A big one. Alex, are you all right?"

Alex blinked a few times and then looked over at me. "I will be fine," he said softly.

It was obvious he was in a light shock. We sat there in silence for another minute. I tried not to think about how I would feel if I were Alex and had killed two people. I wouldn't be handling it even as well as he was. To try to stop my mind going over and over what had happened, I concentrated on the room.

There seemed to be nothing that would make it special. It was as lush as any of the first-class rooms on the *Titanic*. But I couldn't spot one extra panel or closet. Absolutely nothing. We had probably guessed wrong—there wasn't one main device in the center. Yet, why would they guard this room? And why had he

called Susan a Lomax? If she was, why had she even mentioned the Lomax in the first place? Just for one minute I wished I could start getting a few answers to questions instead of getting so damn many new questions.

I turned on the couch so I could see Marjorie and Alex better. Alex looked very pale and his eyes seemed unfocused. Marjorie gave me a half-smile.

"Any suggestions?"

Marjorie slowly shook her head, then squirmed, trying to pull her hands free. "I wish they'd loosen these up. My fingers are starting to hurt."

I pulled on my ties and felt the sharp bite as the twine dug into my skin. I was tempted to get to my feet and somehow try to get the door open. But that seemed utterly fruitless. Chances were both of our captors were outside the door and I wouldn't get farther than a few steps if I tried to make a run for it.

But at the same time, I hated the thought of sitting there waiting for them

---

Some Classic Dean Wesley Smith Stories
Available at your favorite booksellers.

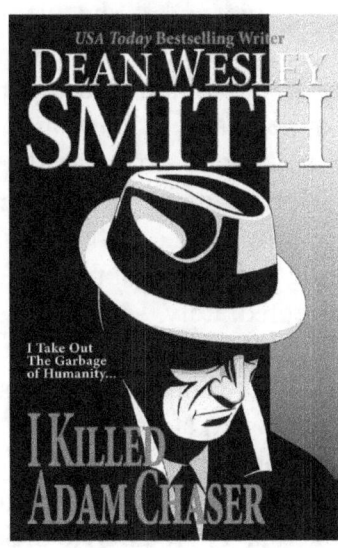

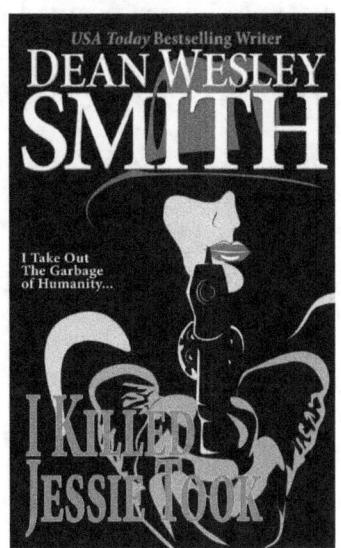

to do whatever they wanted to us. I was just about to suggest to Marjorie and Alex that we try the door, when it opened and both the guard woman and the skeleton man came back in.

He motioned at the couch and then sat down on the bed. The guard woman moved over to Alex. Without the slightest hesitation, she untied his bonds. Then she pulled Marjorie around and untied hers. Her grasp felt strong and tight as she turned me and untied my wrists. She tossed the twine into a corner and moved back over to the door where she stood with her back against it, staring across the room.

I rubbed my wrists and hands, trying to get the blood flowing again. We had just killed one of their people and now we were being untied. Why? This was getting stranger by the minute.

"I'm Patrick," the skeleton man said, giving us a half-smile. "Not my full or complete name, but enough for now. This is Shara." He pointed at the guard woman. She didn't move.

He was trying the "let's-all-be-friends" method, but I wasn't going to go along. I had a hundred questions and it was about time someone started answering them. If he wanted information from us, he was going to have to give a bunch in return.

"I hate games," I said. "So tell me straight off why you untied us."

Patrick smiled. "Because I don't plan on killing you, and it would be impossible to catch you again after the next cycle. So it seems to make more sense to untie you and see if we can talk. So answer a question for me. Why were you trying to free the Lomax?"

"To have her help us get back," Marjorie said.

Patrick leaned back on the bed and laughed. He was so thin it appeared his jaw would become detached from his skull at any moment. It was as if we were watching an animated skull from an old movie.

"Her help you?" he said after a moment. "I'm afraid that would not have been the case, even if it were possible."

"Why?" I asked.

"Because she is a Lomax," he said. "She is here to destroy this group in any way she can. I'm amazed she didn't kill you the first time you met, wherever that was."

Now I laughed a hard, purposeful laugh. "That's what I thought you were," I said. "Why should I believe you any more than her?" She hadn't actually said that, but telling him she had might put him off balance.

"She said that?" he asked. "And when did she tell you that?"

"Before we came through the mirror."

He jumped to his feet, his face tight and very serious. "How long before you came through?"

His sudden action caught me off guard. "Since she got here?" I asked. "Or since she told me?"

He looked over at Shara who also looked very worried. "She would have been able to signal soon after she discovered the mirror," Shara said to Patrick in answer to the unasked question.

"When did she discover the mirror device?" Patrick demanded. "She's been here for nine cycles. That's what we were going by. We assumed she came through immediately."

"I brought the mirror up out of the water twenty-four hours before that."

Patrick looked at Shara.

She shook her head. "They might already have it, depending on where the device was found in relation to their base."

Patrick looked back at me. "Where is the device located?"

"I assume you mean the mirror. It's about a day's travel into the Idaho primitive area. A very remote region."

Patrick nodded. "Then we've got at least this cycle."

"For what?" I didn't like the sound of what he was saying. Fred and Constance would be guarding that mirror. I sure didn't want them in the middle of any war.

"Time," Patrick said, "before the Lomax team Susan undoubtedly called to get to where you left the mirror. We can only hope our people will be able to trace us and arrive here before they get there. If not, we will have to make this fight alone."

"I have friends guarding that mirror. What will happen to them?"

Patrick's face twisted but held its cold look. "I doubt if they will be able to stop them. The Lomax are very efficient. They need that mirror to send a squad against us. Your friends will be fighting maybe six or seven like her."

"Fighting? How can I trust what you are saying any more than I should have trusted what Susan told me?"

Patrick shrugged. "Don't, then. I've untied you. You are free to go anytime you would like. But tell me, will your friends try to protect your mirror?"

I imagined Constance and Fred sitting in their lodge. That mirror was their only link with me. They would protect it with their lives. I would do the same if the situation was reversed. "Yes," I said.

"How many of them are there?"

"Three," I said.

Patrick shook his head slowly. "I'm sorry, but I doubt if they will have much luck against the Lomax. Lomax are a very cold and cruel people. They are called the Ice People for more reasons than their white hair."

"Then we've got to get back and warn them."

Patrick sighed. "I'm afraid that that's not going to be easy." He glanced up at Shara and then back at me.

"You mean you don't have a way back either?" Marjorie said.

Patrick shook his head.

"Did Susan?" I asked.

"The Lomax? No, she didn't either." Patrick stood, went to Shara, and whispered in her ear. She nodded and he turned and faced us. "I wasn't planning on showing you this, but it seems I may need your help in defending this ship."

He moved around the couch to a section of oak paneling on the bow wall. With a few light touches, the paneling slid silently back.

He motioned for us to come closer and Marjorie and I both moved over beside him.

In my life I had seen a lot of things that were so amazing or special that it, as the old saying goes, took my breath away. Usually, it occurred when I looked across a mountain range at sunset, or when I stood in front of a piece of fine art. I suppose it was a deep feeling of appreciation for something that goes beyond everyday beauty. As I stood in front of that open panel, I again felt that same deep, open-mouthed sense of wonder.

The area behind the panel was a deep black, with no visible corners or walls. It was as if I was looking into a huge, completely black room. Suspended waist high and what appeared to be only a few feet inside the blackness was a bluish tinted, crystal-clear replica of the *Titanic*.

I took a moment to simply stare at the fantastic beauty of the floating ship before I started to look at its details. It was at least ten feet long and three feet high, with the starboard side facing us. Every detail was there, yet completely see-through. I could look down through the boat deck into the first-class lounge. I could see the very booth Marjorie and I had sat in. I could see the shelves of books in the library and each step of the grand staircase.

That alone would have been enough, but hundreds of tiny globes of green light, single or in groups, dotted the insides of the ship. Some of the tiny balls floated slowly through the ship. Six green globes filled the small room beside the one bright white dot in the center of the ship. For a moment I stared at the tiny green globe that symbolized where I stood.

"The main time device that keeps us cycling?" I finally asked.

"Yes," Patrick said. "I'm afraid so."

"This is a time machine?" Marjorie asked.

Patrick nodded without looking away from the model ship.

"Amazing," Alex said from behind me. I glanced back at him. A little color seemed to have returned to his cheeks. A good sign. Marjorie reached out and squeezed his arm.

I turned back to gaping at the beautiful blue ship with its tiny globes. "I assume," I said after another minute of silence, "that you are from the future."

Patrick looked over at me. "Why would you say that?"

"Susan admitted she was," I said. "You being from the future, too, would seem to make as much sense as anything. Isn't this similar to your time devices?"

Patrick shook his head and looked back at the suspended ship. "Nothing at all, I'm afraid. This is as far ahead of us

as one of your airlines would be to a covered wagon."

I kept staring at the suspended ship and the green globes. It looked so simple, yet so amazingly complex. "Is there any indication how this hooks up to the mirrors?"

"None that we have found," Patrick said.

"You mean there's no machinery?" Marjorie asked. "Just this?"

Again Patrick nodded.

"And therefore not much hope of finding a way to reverse the mirrors and send us back through. Right?"

Patrick shrugged. "There might have been, given enough time. Lawrence felt he was making headway. But we don't have the time."

He sighed and continued staring at the beautiful ship and the tiny floating green globes, all floating in the pure blackness.

"And now we don't have Lawrence."

To be continued...

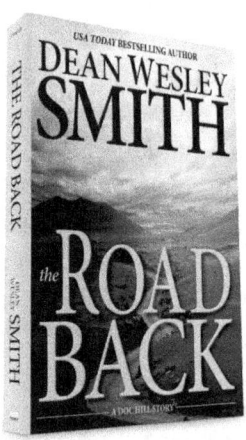

Now Available
from all your favorite booksellers
in trade paper and electronic editions.

Now Available
from all your favorite booksellers
in trade paper and electronic editions.

FREEZEOUT

A COLD POKER GANG MYSTERY

DEAN WESLEY SMITH

USA TODAY BESTSELLING AUTHOR

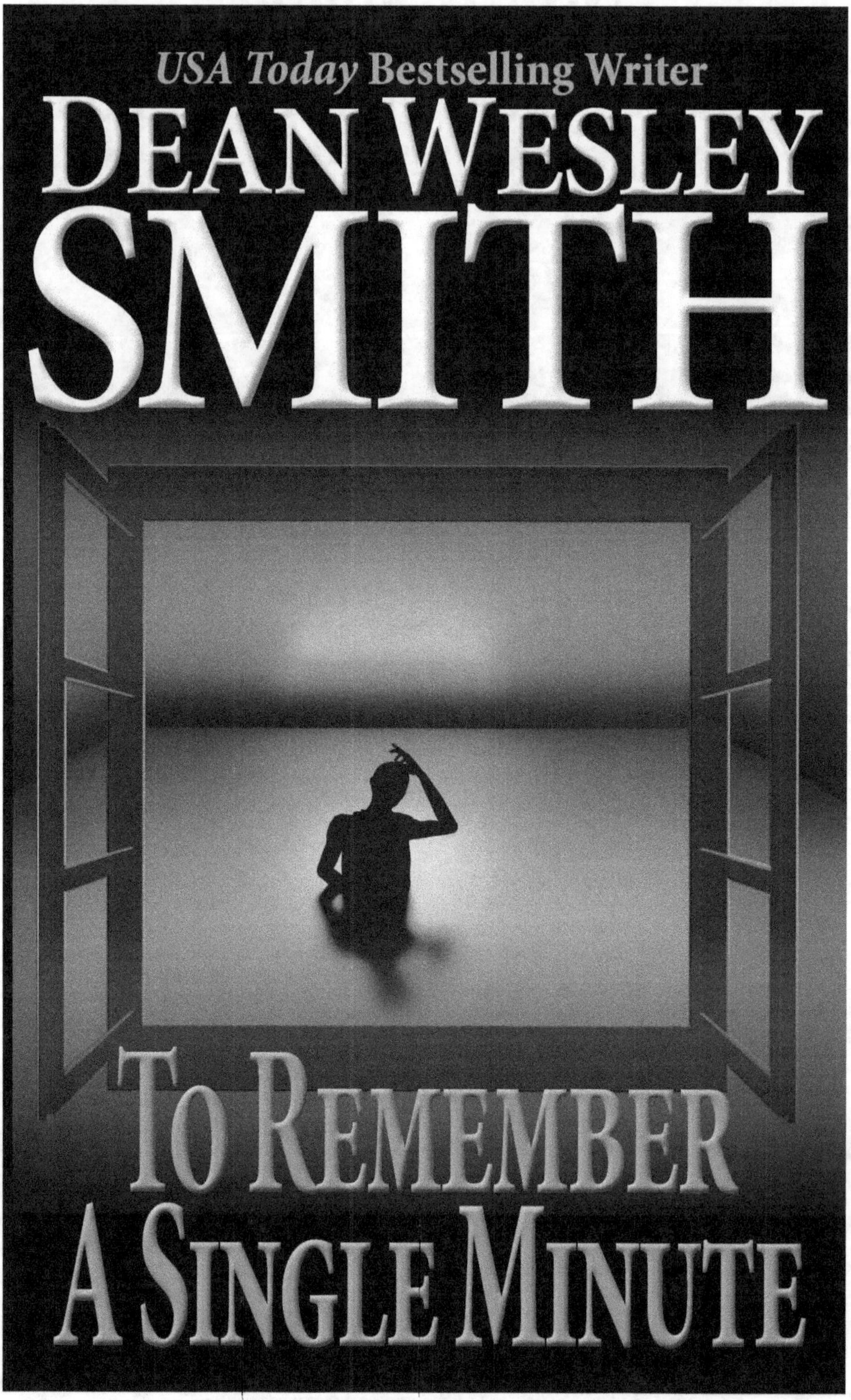
USA Today Bestselling Writer
DEAN WESLEY
SMITH
TO REMEMBER
A SINGLE MINUTE

Remember Incorporated. A company that promises that once the disease took Mike Hanley's mind, he would remember one single minute of his life in stark clarity.

Any minute.

He just needs to pick the minute.

But of all the wonderful minutes in his entire life, which one can he pick?

A science fiction story with a haunting question.

TO REMEMBER A SINGLE MINUTE

ONE

MIKE HANLEY STARED at the sign over the large double glass doors tucked into the impressive gray stone building.

Remember Incorporated

People were coming and going through the doors under the sign like any normal business office.

He stood across the street, his back against the wall of another building, just watching, trying to keep his old and frail body from being trampled by office workers in a hurry to get somewhere.

When he was younger, he had always been in a hurry as well. He couldn't remember where exactly he was in a hurry to go on any given day, but he remembered the sensation of always being in that state of mind.

The day around him was warm, not hot, just warm, and the sidewalks on both sides of the busy four-lane street were crowded with all types, almost all wearing in one form or another the traditional New York black.

He loved this city. He had lived here his entire life.

That morning in his little retirement apartment bedroom, he had combed what was left of his gray hair, had donned a brown Ben Hogan-style golf hat, a new pair of blue slacks, and a loud orange shirt with dark blue suspenders. He knew he looked more like a clown than an eighty-nine-year-old man, but he didn't care and it would make no difference.

He would never remember today.

The instructions that *Remember Incorporated* had given him were clear. He needed to pick one minute of his life to remember before he walked through the door.

And the memory had to be a clear one, sharp, usable.

One minute. Only one minute. That was so unfair.

As an architect and avid outdoors person, he had lived a full life, teeming with millions of minutes he wanted to remember and standing there on the sidewalk, he could remember every one of them like they were yesterday.

He and Carol had had a wonderful fifty-five years together, raising three fantastic kids that he loved more than anything. All of that time was full of minutes worth remembering as well.

He stood for a moment, smiling, remembering all the good times.

Of course, along the way there were a lot of minutes he didn't want to remember

as well, including the minute Carol died last fall. Nothing had been the same since, and when he got the diagnosis that he would be losing his memories fairly quickly over the next few months, he wanted to try to save something of his life.

Remember Incorporated had told him that they could save one minute of his memories for him.

A minute he could always remember. Even when his disease took him down.

A minute would be better than nothing.

Remember Incorporated did it for free. No cost, just a service they provided for seniors such as himself. So no scam, no tricks, nothing.

They offered him one minute.

But from a full, rich life with a million memories all flooding at him as he stood there on the sidewalk, which minute could he pick?

Maybe it was just better to let them all go.

TWO

MIKE HANLEY STARED at the sign over the large double glass doors tucked into the impressive gray stone building.

Remember Incorporated

People were coming and going through the doors under the sign like any normal business office.

He stood across the street, his back against the wall of another building, just watching, trying to keep his old and frail body from being trampled by office workers in a hurry to get somewhere.

When he was younger, he had always been in a hurry as well. He couldn't remember where exactly he was in a hurry to go on any given day, but he remembered the sensation of always being in that state of mind.

The day around him was warm, not hot, just warm, and the sidewalks on both sides of the busy four-lane street were crowded with all types, almost all wearing in one form or another the traditional New York black.

He loved this city. He had lived here his entire life.

That morning in his little retirement apartment bedroom, he had combed what was left of his gray hair, had donned a brown Ben Hogan-style golf hat, a new pair of blue slacks, and a loud orange shirt with dark blue suspenders. He knew he looked more like a clown than an

eighty-nine-year-old man, but he didn't care and it would make no difference.

He would never remember today.

The instructions that *Remember Incorporated* had given him were clear. He needed to pick one minute of his life to remember before he walked through the door.

"Dad?" the voice said, cutting through his memory.

The memory drifted into the background like smoke Mike couldn't seem to hold onto.

"Dad, are you awake?"

Mike Hanley glanced up at the face of a smiling man who had called him dad. He had no idea who the person was. Or even what a dad was, for that matter.

"I'm awake," Mike said.

"I brought you some lunch," the man said, sitting down beside him and helping him get hold of the thing with three points on it. The man helped Mike with what he

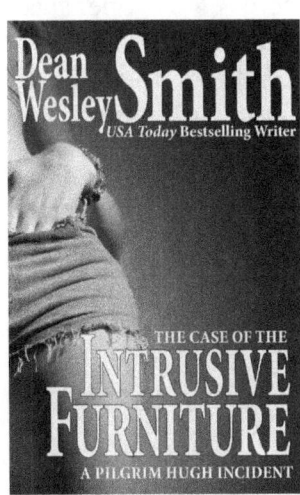

called lunch, then wiped off his face and took the tray away.

Mike watched him go, not really remembering why the man had been there in the first place.

Everything was so puzzling to Mike. He felt at times that he should know something or someone, but just didn't.

He closed his eyes and a memory came flooding back in like smoke filling an empty balloon.

Mike was staring at the sign over the large double glass doors tucked into the impressive gray stone building.

Remember Incorporated

People were coming and going through the doors under the sign like any normal business office.

He stood across the street, his back against the wall of another building, just watching, trying to keep his old and frail body from being trampled by office workers in a hurry to get somewhere.

When he was younger, he had always been in a hurry as well. He couldn't remember where exactly he was in a hurry to go on any given day, but he remembered the sensation of always being in that state of mind.

The day around him was warm, not hot, just warm, and the sidewalks on both sides of the busy four-lane street were crowded with all types, almost all wearing in one form or another the traditional New York black.

He loved this city. He had lived here his entire life.

That morning in his little retirement apartment bedroom, he had combed what was left of his gray hair, had donned a brown Ben Hogan-style golf hat, a new pair of blue slacks, and a loud orange shirt with dark blue suspenders. He knew he looked more like a clown than an eighty-nine-year-old man, but he didn't care and it would make no difference.

He would never remember today.

The instructions that *Remember Incorporated* had given him were clear. He needed to pick one minute of his life to remember before he walked through the door.

And the memory had to be a clear one, sharp, usable.

One minute. Only one minute.

That was so unfair.

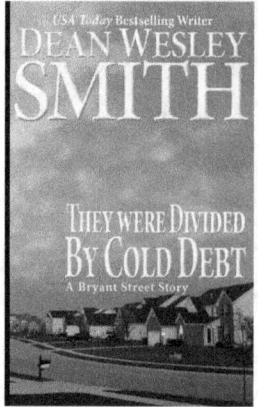

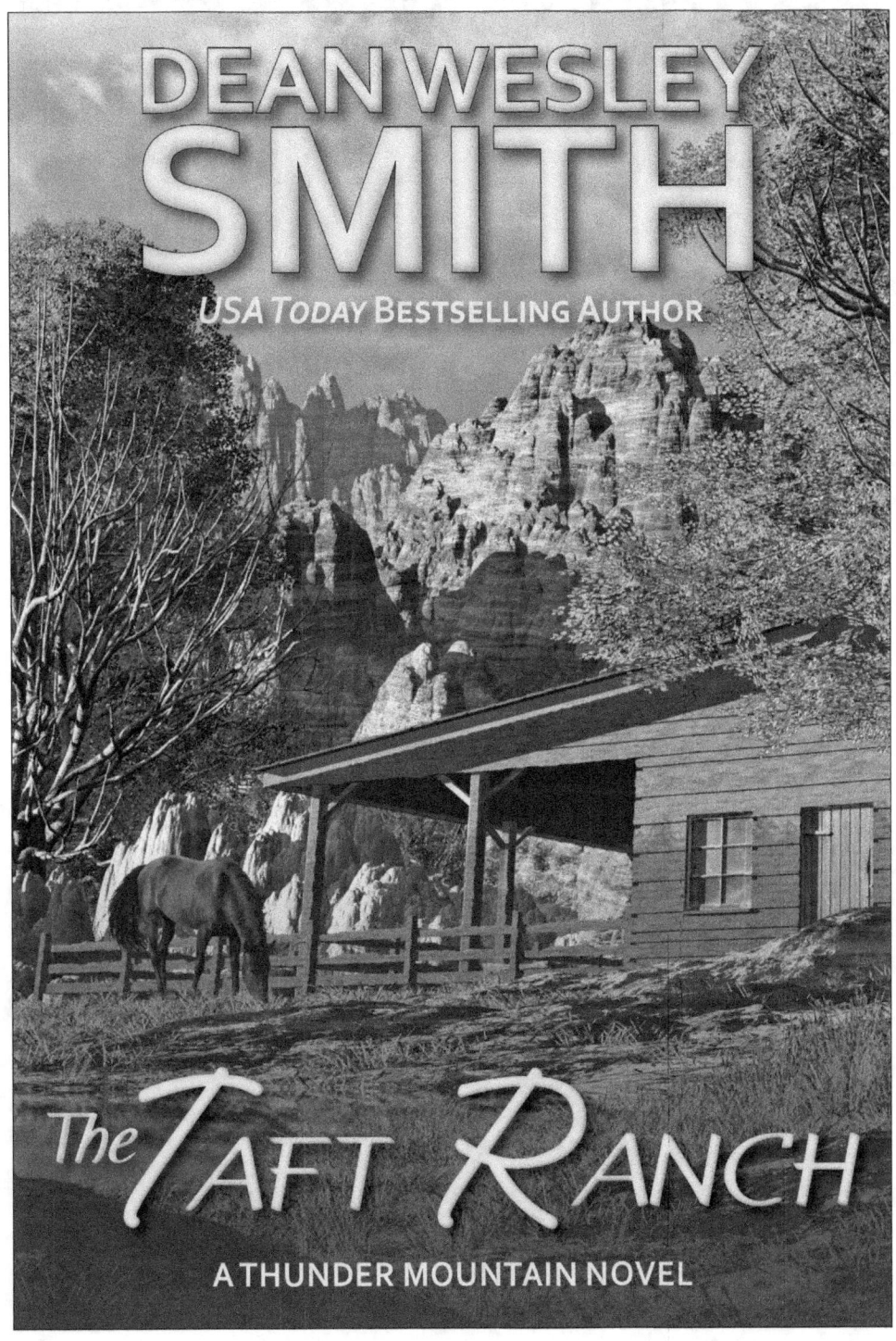

USA *Today* Bestselling Writer

DEAN WESLEY SMITH

A Beautiful Ghost,
A Hunk of a Cop.
Sex? That's the Question.

NOBODY SLEPT HERE

A Ghost of a Chance Story

How can a ghost make love to a live superhero?

Ghost of a Chance Agent Eve Bryson really, really wants to figure that out.

Superhero Deputy Cascade wonders the same thing.

A ghost and a superhero in love. They share everything except sex. What to do?

NOBODY SLEPT HERE
A Ghost of a Chance Story

ONE

HOW CAN A ghost make love to a live superhero?

That was the problem that Ghost of a Chance Agent Eve Bryson and superhero Deputy McCall Cascade had been trying to figure out for their first week as a team.

They shared everything. As a ghost, she could be inside anyone's head and she loved to be inside his head. When she was, he could read all her thoughts as well, her wants and loves and hates.

And she knew all of his.

She had never known someone as well as she knew Cascade after just one week.

In the very short time they had been together, she had fallen completely in love with this man, and she knew he had fallen in love with her. Even though she was dead.

Now, after a week of riding around together in his patrol car helping people, saving a few lives, and spending every day together including breakfast, lunch, and dinner, they were both wanting to take the relationship to the next level.

But for a ghost and a superhero, what exactly was the next level?

He could see her just fine, but they couldn't really touch each other. Granted, being in each other's minds was pretty damn nifty as far as she was concerned, but they were both very, very horny.

So far they had managed to avoid it because they had no answer to how to have a physical relationship. But Eve knew they had to solve this very, very frustrating problem.

And fast.

So on Saturday afternoon, the first day Cascade had off work as a sheriff's deputy, Eve decided to go try to get some answers.

Cascade was stretched out in front of the television by 9 in the morning in his apartment, and she had no doubt he would be asleep in ten minutes. Having a ghost in his head for an entire week had been tiring. He hadn't been a superhero much longer than she had been a ghost, so all this was new for both of them.

She was tired as well. But the sex thing needed to get solved.

She had set up a meeting with Jewel and her boyfriend, Tommy, at their normal breakfast place, the Golden Nugget Buffet in Las Vegas. So with an air kiss to her partner, she jumped from outside Portland, Oregon, to Vegas.

Tommy had been a cop when alive and Jewel a doctor. They were the two Ghost of a Chance agents that had trained her in what she could do as an agent in this new life, and she had called Jewel a couple of times the first week for different forms of help.

This morning, Jewel had on a beautiful blue blouse and had her long brown hair pulled back off her face. Tommy had on a T-shirt with a light shirt over it. With his close-cut brown hair, he reminded Eve a lot of Cascade.

Both of them were tall and exercised every day a great deal, mostly running.

Jewel and Tommy had both died in a car wreck as she had done. They had just met and as a deputy, he was driving Jewel, as a doctor, to an emergency in the Montana mountains when a deer jumped in front of them and they had hit a tree.

As had happened to Eve, instead of crossing over, Jewel had remained in this real world and been recruited as a Ghost of a Chance Agent. Jewel and Tommy had been recruited as agents together and had fallen in love.

Eve liked Jewel and Tommy a great deal and felt as if she could trust them with anything.

They had already finished their breakfast and were sipping on coffee when she arrived.

Ghosts could eat without a problem. Everything on the planet had a ghost element to it. Clothing, food, you name it. And food tasted wonderful, just wonderful as a ghost. You could take, say, an apple, the ghost element of the apple, and the real-world apple would still remain. And that ghost element, the essence of the apple, tasted like the best apple in the world no matter what.

So eating had become in one week one of her real pleasures in being dead, besides being with Cascade. And being able to read other people's thoughts and walk through things. That was all fun as well, but mostly she just loved every minute with Cascade.

Jewel and Tommy were much later morning people than she and Cascade were, because of his job schedule. Jewel and Tommy had just finished breakfast, for her it was getting closer to lunch.

The Golden Nugget had a wonderful feel about it. Brown cloth decorations, brown oak wood, and large windows looking out over the pool gave the place a feeling of relaxation instead of Las Vegas hurry-up-and-spend of so many of the casinos.

There were only about twenty live humans scattered around the large room and Jewel and Tommy had a table off to one side near a planter. It seemed that they always had that table. Live humans never sat there.

When Eve had trained here in Vegas after her death, she and Jewel and Tommy had spent a lot of time right here in this buffet at the same table.

The smell of bacon and waffles filled the air and even though she had eaten a few hours before, she went for a waffle as dessert. Damn she was loving to eat, but Jewel had warned Eve that she had better get exercising fairly quickly. It seemed that ghosts could gain weight, and with as good as food tasted, Eve could see how it wouldn't be hard to stack on the pounds.

Eve joined Jewel and Tommy and they asked about her and Cascade's first week and she filled them in as she worked on her waffle.

"I sometimes miss just riding on patrol," Tommy said. "It was always a combination of quiet boredom combined at times with acute awareness and broken by moments of panicked action."

"Would you leave this life for that again?" Jewel asked him.

He laughed. "Not a chance."

All three of them laughed, then Jewel focused on Eve. "So what's the problem?"

Eve took a deep breath, trying to figure out where to start. Then she decided to just tell them what was happening instead of asking questions around the problem.

"Cascade and I have fallen in love," she said.

"Wow, that's wonderful to hear," Jewel said, smiling a huge grin.

"It will sure make spending all those hours together a lot more fun," Tommy said, also smiling.

"It is fun," Eve said. "More than either of us have ever experienced before. We are sharing things I didn't know I would ever share with anyone else. And he's just an amazingly special person."

"So what's the problem?" Jewel asked.

Tommy laughed and looked at his partner, shaking his head at Jewel. "Sex."

"Oh," Jewel said, suddenly sitting back as she realized Eve's problem.

"Yeah," Eve said. "The problem, put bluntly, is that Cascade and I are beyond horny and damned if we can figure out the ghost-and-alive-connection problem."

"Oh," Jewel said again.

Eve pushed the remains of her waffle away. From Jewel's reaction, this was not going to be an easy problem to solve.

If there was a solution at all.

TWO

"**WE NEED SOME** help with this one," Jewel said.

Tommy nodded.

And before Eve could stop Jewel or even ask who the help might be, Jewel said into the air, "K.J., a little help."

"Need a minute to finishing getting dressed if you don't mind." A voice in the air above the table seemed to echo from a deep chamber.

Eve looked around, but, of course, no one was there.

Jewel turned to Eve. "K.J. is our team's boss. He is the one who reports to the gods and he is the one who gets us our assignments, unlike you and Cascade who just go out and save people."

"Good thinking," Tommy said to Jewel. "K.J. has been dead for over a hundred years and has a reputation as a party person."

"One of the best, if not *the* best party person," a man said, appearing next to the table. "Please, if you must spread my reputation, do it with some accuracy."

The guy was short, really, really short, wearing a gray pinstriped silk suit and vest, a pink tie with flamingos on it, pink slippers, and a bright pink feathery hat that had a tail on it that went down his back.

Eve just stared, her mouth open. Her life in Oregon had been sheltered, clearly.

He bowed slightly to Eve, the feathers in his hat flowing around him. "I am K.J. I have heard you are a fast study."

"I had good instructors," Eve managed to say, nodding to Tommy and Jewel.

K.J. glanced at the buffet, then looked at Jewel. "Before I move to get some maple syrup on this grand tie, what is your problem?"

Now Available
**from all your favorite booksellers
in trade paper and electronic editions**.

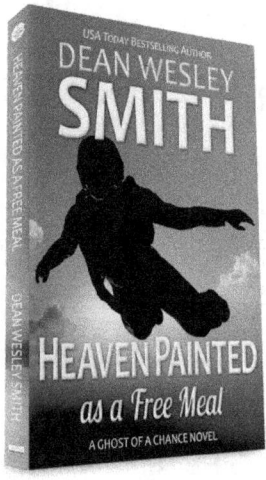

Jewel indicated that K.J. should sit down at the table.

"A major issue I see," K.J. said, sitting.

"You have heard," Jewel said, "that Eve is the first ghost agent to partner with a live superhero."

"How is that going?" K.J. said. "A grand experiment, if I must say."

"We are doing well," Eve said. "Saved some lives so far."

"And that is why we are here in this ghostly state," K.J. said, nodding.

"But Eve and her partner, Deputy McCall Cascade, have a problem," Jewel said.

"You are with Cascade?" K.J. said, his eyes lighting up.

Eve was surprised, because in all the times inside of Cascade's head, she had never seen a thought about this sparklingly-dressed ghost. She was sure she would have remembered. And positive Cascade would have remembered K.J. as well.

"I am," she said.

"Oh, girl, how do you keep your hands off of that hunk of a man?" K.J. asked. "I saw his picture when he was recruited and got so hot I had to retire for the day and take care of issues."

Eve was fairly certain her face was bright red.

Jewel and Tommy were both laughing.

"That's the problem we called you here about," Jewel finally said.

"I can see no problem at all with climbing all over that hunk of a man," K.J. said. He looked at Eve. "Is it dreamy to be riding with him in his masculine patrol car with all the leather seats and the wonderful tools of manhood?"

She blushed again and laughed. "It is dreamy, yes."

"I knew it would be," K.J. said, clapping his hands. "Just knew it. You are one lucky ghost, girl."

"I think so," Eve said.

"So," Jewel said, between laughter. "How do they go about having sex?"

K.J. looked at Jewel, then back to Eve with a sly grin on his face.

"Oh, girl, you are a fast mover, aren't you?"

THREE

EVE FIGURED HER face was about as red as it was going to get, so she smiled at K.J. Then said, "Do you blame me?"

"Oh, my, not at all," K.J. said, fanning himself.

Eve thought Tommy was going to fall out of his chair laughing.

Jewel was trying to hold it together enough to actually get an answer out of K.J.

Eve was really starting to like this crazy ghost of a boss.

"So, what is needed," Jewel asked, "for these two to have sex? Real sex."

"Passion," K.J. said, "but with that hunk of a man, I doubt that is your problem, is it?"

"It is not," Eve said, smiling at him. "And it is not his problem toward me either. We both want this, but both of us are so new to our worlds, we have no idea how to go about that part of a relationship."

"Like two teenagers in the backseat of a car," K.J. said. "The fumbling is half the fun I am told."

"All I remember is the fear and the worry and the sweating," Jewel said.

Again, Tommy just laughed and shook his head.

Eve hadn't had any experience in back seats of cars. And her first sexual experiences hadn't been that rewarding, actually. And her sexual experiences with her loser of a husband hadn't changed that. So with Cascade, she was hoping for a little more.

Actually, a lot more.

K.J. looked at her. "You ever read the fine short story 'Man of Steel, Woman of Kleenex'?"

Eve shook her head. She had no idea what he was talking about.

Again Tommy laughed and Jewel just looked at K.J. with a stern look.

"No?" K.J. asked Eve. "For the better, since even though Cascade is a superhero and someone can put a hand through you like Kleenex, the situation in the story does not apply."

Tommy had to catch himself from laughing himself off his chair. If they hadn't been ghosts, everyone in the place would have been staring at them.

"K.J.," Jewel said, pretending to put on a stern face. "This is a serious problem that these two young lovers are trying to solve."

K.J. was laughing with Tommy at his own joke, but finally nodded and took a moment to catch his breath.

Eve was going to have to look up that story just to see why they were laughing.

Finally K.J. looked at both Jewel and Tommy. "I will teach you all a very nifty trick that none of your team knows yet, but that might come in handy at times."

He glanced around, clearly to make sure none of the live customers were watching, even though none of the four of them could be seen. Then K.J. reached forward and picked up the Keno ticket holder in the center of the table.

Not just the ghost element of the ticket holder, but the entire holder.

Then he set it down on the table with an audible click, smiling.

"Damn," Tommy said. "How did you do that?"

K.J. pointed to his head. "Just as we do all of our skills. I just imagined it."

"So we can cross over into the real world without controlling a person to do it for us?" Jewel asked, clearly as stunned as Eve was feeling.

"Within limits," K.J. said. "As far as I know, a normal human can't see us no matter what we do. Something about light and things I didn't understand."

"Cascade can see me fine thanks to Laverne," Eve said.

"Makes sense because he's a super-hero," K.J. said, nodding.

K.J. then stood and indicated all three of them should follow him over to a planter filled with artificial plants that divided the buffet from a small lobby at the top of an escalator.

"Put your hand through the plants," K.J. said to each of them.

They all did.

Eve had gotten used to walking through things and not feeling a thing. She actually kind of liked it.

"Now," K.J. said, "Imagine your hand is solid enough to move a plant leaf."

Eve used what Jewel and Tommy had taught her about imagining being in different places and just being there, and floating, and so on. All of her training had been on using her imagination. It seemed that ghosts felt like they were part of this world, but were not really, so then had what seemed like powers to jump any-where they could imagine or float places or make others do as a ghost wanted.

Ghosts felt like they were tied in this world, but actually were not, thus their imagination had to break them free.

Eve focused that same imagination energy on making her hand solid and touching the plant leaf.

And suddenly she could feel the leaf. Not the ghost element of the leaf, that had a certain feel, but the actual artificial leaf.

It moved under her touch.

Jewel and Tommy had the same success.

"Wonderful! K.J. said, clapping his hands like a teenager happy to see someone.

He turned and went back to the table. As he did, Eve watched him study the room to make sure no one was looking, then he pulled out a chair that was tucked in too close to the table.

Not the ghost part of the chair, but the actual chair.

To any live person watching, either in the restaurant or on a camera, that chair must have looked like it had moved by itself.

Jewel, Tommy, and Eve tried to move a chair, but even though they all could feel the chair's surface, they couldn't get enough grip or energy to move it.

"This takes time and practice to learn," K.J. said as they all sat back down.

Then he turned to Eve. "But I have discovered over the years, after many pleasurable nights in my oversized hot tub with wonderful and very-much-alive superheroes who could see me, the prac-tice is very much worth the effort."

Eve was again convinced she was blushing.

"That's how you and Madge from the diner did it," Tommy said, smiling.

Eve figured he was clearly talking about an event before she had died. She would ask later.

"A fella doesn't kiss and tell," K.J. said, laughing.

Jewel just laughed and shook her head.

"If I can make my hand solid to touch something," Eve asked, "can I make other parts of my body solid as well for Cascade's touch?"

K.J. smiled and fanned himself again with an imaginary fan. "With practice, Mr. Hunk Cascade can feel any part of you that you would want him to feel."

Eve was about to jump up and down for joy.

She smiled at Jewel and Tommy. "Thank you both."

Then she stood and moved over and kissed K.J. solidly on the cheek.

"And thank you," Eve said to K.J. "And now I need to go do some practicing on Cascade's wonderful and very masculine body."

"I think I might have the vapors just thinking of that," K.J. said, again fanning himself.

She laughed and jumped back to Cascade's apartment.

He was stretched out on the couch, sound asleep. She knelt by the couch and then gently touched his face.

The light stubble on his cheeks felt wonderful against her hand.

He stirred as she brushed his cheek again. He smiled and opened his eyes.

"That felt wonderful," he said, looking into her eyes.

"It did," she said.

"How?" he asked.

"I'll explain it all later," she said.

Then she stood and stripped off her clothes as he watched intently. Quickly she was standing there in front of him completely naked and enjoying his look.

All he could do was stare.

Finally he said, "You are so beautiful."

She imagined her hand firm and reached out for his hand.

"Come on," she said, actually feeling his hand solidly in hers as she pulled him to his feet. "We have some practicing to do."

"What kind of practicing?" he asked, smiling.

"The best kind," she said. "The very best."

~

Some Classic Dean Wesley Smith Stories
Available at your favorite booksellers.

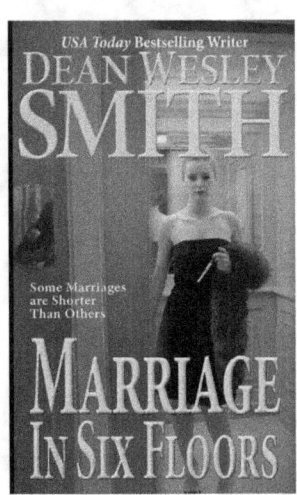

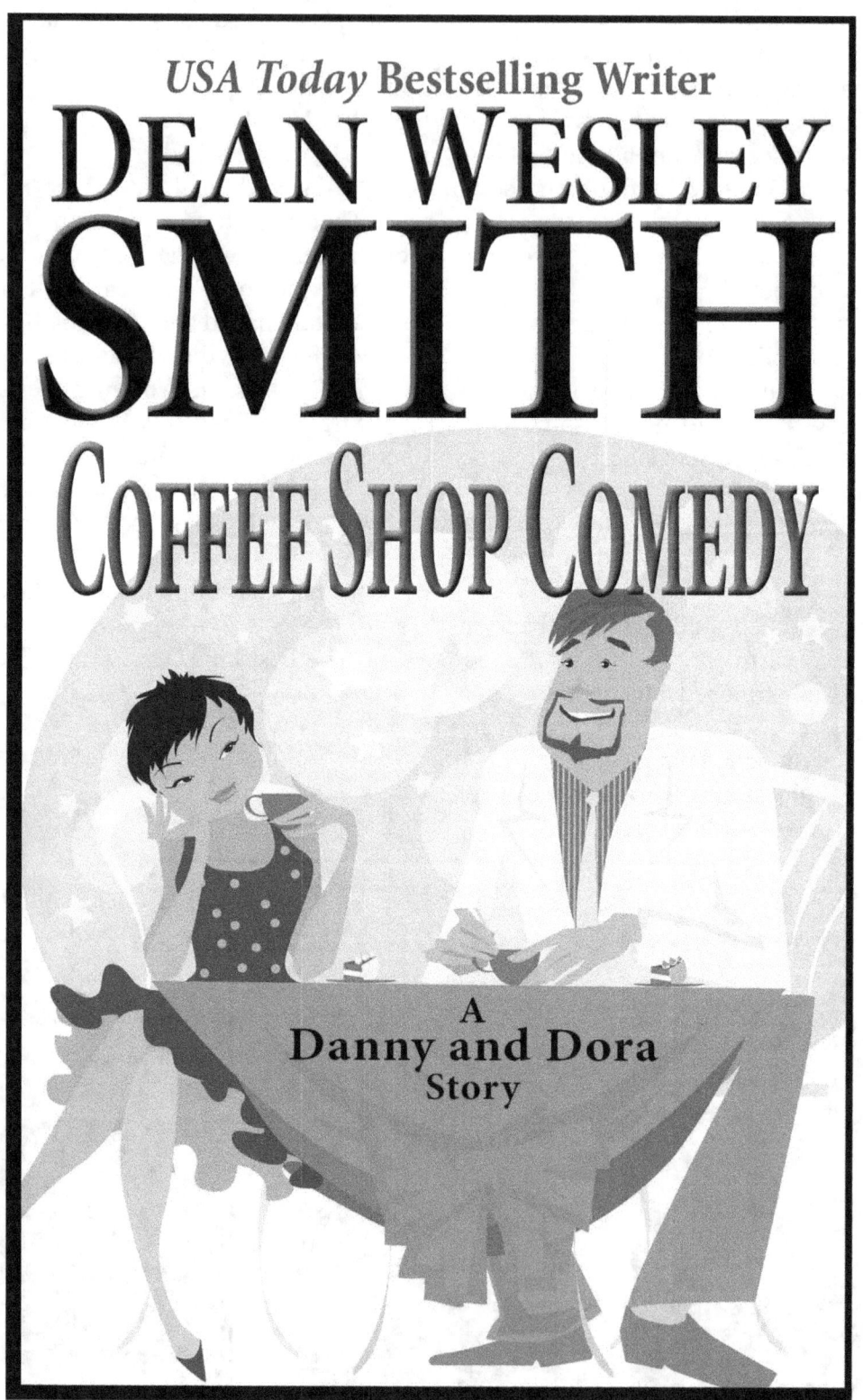

USA *Today* Bestselling Writer

DEAN WESLEY SMITH

COFFEE SHOP COMEDY

A
Danny and Dora
Story

Danny needs a voice.

Dora needs a way to deliver her jokes besides selling them to other comics.

Both write and love comedy. Both love coffee. Their attraction catches them both by surprise. Can they solve each other's problems?

The origin story of the famous crime-solving comedy team, Danny and Dora.

COFFEE SHOP COMEDY
A Danny and Dora Story

ONE

DANNY MCDOW needed a voice.

Not that he couldn't speak. He could. Just like any other guy, words came out of his mouth and people heard them.

But the problem was his words were plain. He spoke like a machine, but actually machines spoke with more interest than he did. With a machine, you knew a machine was talking.

When Danny spoke, his tone was flat, his words clear, and nothing at all was distinct.

Made it damn near impossible to tell a funny story. And that's where Danny's problem was. He wanted to be a comedian.

He loved to laugh, he loved to entertain, but comedians had voices. They could punctuate their jokes with slight tone rises. Or emphasis. Or even a conspiracy whisper.

No matter how hard Danny practiced, he couldn't do any of those things. His voice was flat, dull, and in his ears, lifeless.

And that was killing him.

In the real world, Danny was anything but lifeless. A much sought-after business lawyer, Danny always wore silk three-piece suits, drove a Porsche from his million-dollar home in the hills to his office building that he owned. His personal office was on the top floor of a twenty-story downtown Portland building.

He knew from the start of his legal career while still in Harvard that with his voice, he could never walk into court. He would put a jury or a judge to sleep while trying to be passionate. So he made sure his clients always won outside of court, with settlements of record proportions that just made him even richer than he already was.

His clients found his voice soothing after they got used to it. He had a reputation of never getting excited or mad, even though at times he had been feeling both emotions. It just never showed in his voice.

Ever.

At night, while at home alone in his massive mansion, he sat in his home theater and studied comedians for hours and hours. He spent even more hours every night in his home office, dressed in jeans and an old sweatshirt, writing notebooks full of material for a stand-up routine he would never get a chance to do.

And he even practiced and memorized some of the routines. But when he recorded them, they just fell flat.

He was a successful lawyer, one of the best. But the law had never been his dream. Comedy was his dream.

But with his voice, he had no idea how to go about it.

He needed a voice. And a voice was something not even his money could buy.

TWO

THE DAY DANNY met Dora Patton was a warm spring day in May. The weather in Portland had been clear and the sky blue. The volcanoes were out, as

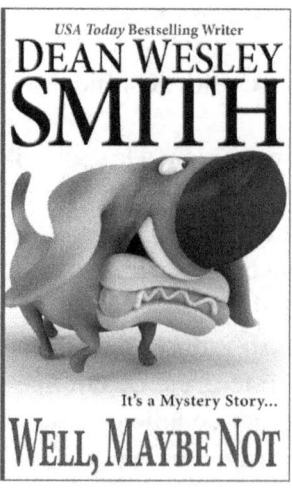

they say in Portland when you could see a number of the nearby volcanoes and their snow-covered peaks in the Cascade Mountains. Days like this were one of the many reasons he had come home to Oregon to practice law.

Danny parked his Porsche that morning a little after nine in his parking spot under his building. On the way in, his assistant had called and told him his ten o'clock appointment had cancelled.

So he took off his tie and jacket and left them in his car, then grabbed a notebook and headed for a nearby coffee shop, enjoying the walk and watching people because watching people, he knew from all his study of comedy, helped in finding jokes.

When he got to the coffee shop, it wasn't crowded. In fact, besides him, only two other people were there, both with their heads buried in laptops at tables near windows, tapping away. One was a guy with a beard and bald spot on the top of his head, the other was a woman about his age of mid-thirties from what he could tell without seeing her face and eyes.

She had short brown hair that had clearly been styled.

More than likely both were writers like him. He knew that writers loved coffee shops for some reason. He actually did as well.

This morning the coffee shop smelled of rich coffee and some kind of cookies that had just been baked.

The two people behind the counter stopped their cleaning chores long enough to get him a double mocha, then he found a table and chair near a window, opened up his notebook to a fresh page, titled it with the date and the location, and then sat back, thinking.

He had no idea how long he had been in that position when the woman who had been at one of the laptops said to him, "You need to move around more."

He jerked and looked up into beautiful green eyes and a broad smile. He had been right, she was about his age and wore a large University of Oregon green sweatshirt and jeans. And she was stunningly beautiful. The short brown hair really shaped her face perfectly.

"Excuse me," he said.

"Oh, I like your voice," she said, smiling. "I just noticed you hadn't moved and as a writer, you need to move around at times or it causes back and other health issues."

Danny nodded, then realized what she had said.

"You like my voice?" he asked.

"Modulated perfectly right in the middle range," she said.

He blinked, doing his best to get his bearings. Then he said, "Please, join me for a few minutes."

He pointed to the other chair.

"My name is Danny."

He didn't tell her his last name because just up the block was his building with McDow Building plastered in large letters on the side and over the front door.

"I'm Dora," she said, extending her hand and smiling that wonderful smile that could light up a room. "Great to meet you."

She sat down. "I have a minute or so to talk with another writer before I need to get back to work."

"What kind of writing do you do?" he asked.

"Comedy," she said. "I write for different comedians, selling them routines."

He damn near choked. "Seriously?"

"Great fun," she said, nodding.

"Do you perform?" he asked.

She shook her head and he could tell she was sad about that. "Just haven't figured out a way to get over the fear of getting up on a stage alone. Working on it, though."

The smile came back into her eyes. "What kind of writing do you do?"

"Comedy," he said, smiling.

"You're just saying that," she said.

"Seriously," he said. He slid his notebook toward her and turned it around so she could see. "Flip back and you'll see some of the routines I've been working on."

She did and then after a moment shook her head and laughed and slid his notebook back to him.

"This is just very strange," she said. "I pegged you for a novelist. A rich one from the looks of your shirt and vest and haircut."

"Disappointed?" he asked.

"Not in the slightest," she said. "Novelists are boring people because they just live inside their own heads most of the time."

"Never met one," Danny said. "So wouldn't know."

"Trust me," she said. "So you perform?"

"With this voice?" He shook his head. "I have some sort of defect that won't allow me to have inflections or tonal changes or anything in my voice."

"I like your voice," she said.

"Don't say soothing," he said, smiling at her.

At that moment his phone rang and he glanced at it before turning it off.

"I have an appointment I have to make," he said. "Thus the clothes."

She actually looked disappointed.

"If you are up for it," he said, "I would love to meet you here tomorrow morning and talk comedy writing and performing.

I have been studying it since I was in high school and seldom find anyone I can talk to about comedy."

She smiled again. "I would love that."

"Name the time," he said.

"Nine in the morning," she said.

"Until tomorrow," Danny said. "Always leave them laughing."

She actually laughed at that old movie title and said, "I'll certainly try. But Milton Berle was pretty damn good."

"On the money," he said and headed for the door, impressed she knew the old comedy movie.

The sound of her laugh stayed with him all the way to his office. That laugh alone at one of his stupid jokes made his day.

Maybe his month.

THREE

DANNY HAD CANCELLED all his appointments for the next day. He figured that even if Dora didn't show up, he would use the day to work on his writing. He ran the law firm after all. If he couldn't take a day now and then, who could?

He parked his Porsche in his spot under his building and with his notebook in hand, headed up the street toward the coffee shop. Today he had on his kick-around-the-house clothes. Jeans, an older dress shirt with the sleeves rolled up, and tennis shoes.

Dora was already there, working at something on her laptop.

He had a luxury she hadn't had. She had given him her full name so he had his people do a secret search on her. She was smart, a masters degree from the University of Oregon in Human Studies. She was divorced, no kids, and actually did write for some well-known touring comedians.

He had been impressed.

When he entered the coffee shop with its smells of coffee and fresh bread, she looked up and smiled, waved and went back to work as he moved to get his drink.

With drink in hand a couple minutes later, he went back to her table near the window as she closed her laptop and put it in a backpack at her feet.

"Good morning," she said, smiling.

Morning," he said, sitting down. "Hope I'm not disturbing a deadline."

"Nope," she said, smiling and sipping from her coffee. "Cleared that yesterday. I actually was working on an idea that triggered with something you said yesterday."

"Really?" he asked. He couldn't imagine what he had said that triggered anything.

"Could I ask you a couple questions?" she asked. "Feel free to not answer or tell me it's none of my business."

He nodded and smiled. "Fire away."

"Do you really want to perform?"

He took a deep breath, trying to decide how much to tell this beautiful stranger. She was who she said she was, so maybe she had an idea that would get him performing his routines on stage. Or any routine for that matter. After all these years, he wasn't picky.

"More than I would ever admit to anyone but a stranger like you," he said.

She laughed, which made his day. Clearly she liked his dead voice.

"I have to admit," she said, "I want to perform with the same passion. It sometimes kills me to see my routines on a national comedy show being mouthed by someone else. Granted, they paid for them, but still, it's hard."

"I can only imagine," he said. "But at least you are working in comedy. More than I am doing."

She nodded at that.

"I told you yesterday," she said, "that I liked your voice."

"You like sameness?" he asked.

She smiled. "I like consistency, which your voice has. Always the same tone, the same level, the same delivery. And you seem perfectly in control all the time."

"And that is my problem," he said.

"But it wouldn't be if you were on stage with a partner."

Danny blinked at her.

"Burns and Allen," she said, leaning forward, excitement in her voice. "Straight line, punch line. Facial reaction of the straight person. You do great facial reactions. And your voice would be perfect for straight lines tossed to a partner."

He sat there staring at her trying to get his mind around what she was saying.

"Let me show you what I am thinking," she said. "I assume you have the expensive jacket that went with that outfit yesterday."

He nodded.

She reached into her bag and pulled out a blonde wig and put it on. Then she turned to him and blinked her eyes a bunch of times really fast.

She was a completely different person, he had to admit.

"Now imagine me in some tight skirt and awful blouse and a little too much makeup. You know, trailer trash. And you standing there with your silk pinstriped suit. Hell, we'd be a great sight-gag just to start."

He nodded. "I can imagine that clearly, actually."

"And we would write for the gag. I would be Dumb Dora."

"Like the old comic strip," he said, way back?"

She nodded. "Gracie Allen patterned her routine on Dumb Dora. I think we can modernize Burns and Allen and I love that kind of humor that Gracie did."

He sat back, thinking. Then he nodded, feeling more excitement than he wanted to admit to even himself at that moment.

"So what do you think?" she asked, pulling off the wig and putting it back in her pack.

"I love the idea," he said. "I flat love it and it fits perfectly with my voice."

"We would need to set up a back story of some sort," she said, smiling.

He remembered a routine he had written a while back. "How about this? I am a rich detective going around the country solving crimes for rich people, and you play my assistant who actually is the one who solves the crimes by asking nonsense Gracie-like questions."

"Every routine could be a little story?" she said, almost bouncing on the chair in excitement. "I love it. I absolutely love it."

"And it will solve both of our problems about getting on the stage and performing."

"It will," she said, the smile so large, she was beaming.

And he had a hunch he was beaming as well.

"So what do we call this?" he asked. "Dora and Danny?"

"The other way around," she said, shaking her head. "Just like Burns and Allen. Danny and Dora."

He liked that a great deal. More than he wanted to admit.

He reached his hand forward over the table. "Partner?"

"Partner," she said, shaking his hand. "Fifty-fifty split on everything."

"On everything," he said.

Then she laughed. "And I don't even know your last name."

He pointed out the window and down the street. You could see his last name on the building a little over a block away.

She looked where he was pointing, then shook her head. "Missing what you are pointing at."

"My name is Danny McDow. I own that building."

She stared down the street at his tall building for a moment, then broke out laughing. "Now that's funny."

He laughed with her and they went back to working out the details of their partnership.

Then an hour later he really enjoyed her shocked expression when he showed her his office. To him, that was funny.

The only thing she had to say after seeing the view from his office over the city and the river and bridges was, "Guess money for touring clubs won't be an issue."

"Not in the slightest," he said, laughing. "Not in the slightest."

He was about to achieve a life-long dream to work in comedy.

And all because of a chance meeting in a coffee shop.

There was absolutely nothing funny about that. But it sure made him smile.

~

Now Available
from all your favorite booksellers in trade paper and electronic editions.

USA TODAY BESTSELLING AUTHOR

DEAN WESLEY SMITH

STAR FALL

A SEEDERS UNIVERSE NOVEL

USA Today *bestselling writer Dean Wesley Smith returns to his fan-favorite Seeders Universe series with a seventh novel,* Star Fall.

Seeders never do anything in a small way, including their sports. Matt and Carey, the chairmen of the Starburst ship Star Fall *started a yearly relay race from the very front of their ship to the tail and back again. An extreme relay of over nine thousand kilometers run by ten-member teams.*

But before the race could start, a scout ship vanishes inside a shielded galaxy. Who could put a shield around an entire galaxy? And why?

A galaxy-spanning tale of adventure, suspense, and the vast possibilities of space.

STAR FALL
A Seeders Universe Novel

For Kris

SECTION ONE
Lost

PROLOGUE

CHAIRMAN RAY STOOD beside his wife, Chairman Tacita, on the massive bridge of their mother ship, staring at the day's battle reports coming in from hundreds of thousands of light-years of space. Around them the three tiers of stations were all filled with fifty command crew. The noise in the room was low, only a few conversations.

Ray knew they would win this war. He and Tacita both knew that now. It would take a little more time, but they would win.

The fight had gone on now for over three hundred years. It would take another hundred years to mop it all up. A short time in the life of Seeders like them.

Ray's long gray hair hung down his back as he stood staring at the large screen filling one wall that scrolled all the reports. He had on his normal jeans and dress shirt. Tacita had short black hair that seemed to shine and she dressed as she normally did, with dark dress slacks and a silk blouse.

"We can't let this happen again," Tacita said, her voice her normal calm and level tone as she studied the reports.

Ray glanced at his wife, his partner for more hundreds of thousands of years than he wanted to think about. Her short black hair shaped her face, often giving her a stern look he knew didn't usually match her personality. She was still beautiful by any measure. He couldn't imagine living a moment without her.

He stood over six feet tall and didn't really tower over her. They made the perfect couple as far as he was concerned.

"I know we can't," he said. "We can never be caught off guard again by anything going on near human space. Or anywhere in the universe, for that matter."

The alien experiment they had been fighting for the centuries had threatened to overwhelm human space, destroy millions of galaxies full of human life. Only luck and the sheer brilliance of the six chairmen of three ships had saved them.

But now the battle was nearing its end and victory was at hand.

"Do you have any suggestions?" Tacita asked.

"I do," he said. "Please bring up the Starburst image."

The battle map on the big screen in front of them was replaced by what looked like a point of light with lines radiating in three dimensions from it.

"You are going to have to explain this," Tacita said.

"The center point is the Milky Way Galaxy, since that is where we have major construction facilities to build new ships for the war effort."

She nodded to that.

"Each line represents one massive ship," Ray said, "a combination battle ship and scout ship, but far larger than any of our mother ships."

"How much larger?" Tacita asked.

"Each ship should be able to hold over three million souls," Ray said. "And many thousands of scout ships and battleships."

"And their use?" Tacita asked. "I assume you intend for them to go out along these lines. Where do those lines stop?"

"We give every ship the new trans-tunnel drives and they go out five hundred years before moving over and returning on a new course back."

"Five hundred years at those speeds will take all those ships beyond any edge of space we have been able to see," Tacita said, turning to look at her husband.

He nodded. "We need to know what exists in the universe before something like the aliens finds human space."

He pointed to the starburst illustration on the screen. "All of the known universe and far beyond. And that's how we find out."

ONE

CHAIRMAN CAREY NOACK stood beside the large chairmen's chairs in the command center of *Star Fall*. On the massive wall screen in front of her the daily reports were coming in from all the scout ships. She knew that if anything was abnormal, *Star Fall* would report it to her. But she still liked to scan the reports every day. Habit built out of hundreds of years now of doing the same thing.

At least now the reports weren't about war, but about exploring galaxies. She liked this a lot better.

Carey stood not much over five-four, had long brown hair she kept pulled back, and always wore jeans, a light blouse, and tennis shoes. Even though she had lived now for a very long time, she still looked not a day over thirty. And was still in as good of shape as she had been when she met Matt Ladel all those years ago in the dead Earth city of Portland.

Living seemingly forever was a real bonus about being a Seeder.

Around her the other twenty members of the main command crew were all busy working as well. The command center was exactly the same as the old *Star Fall*

command center had been, even though the new ship was ten times the size of the older ship.

She was glad she and Matt had decided to keep the command center looking the same on the new ship. Over the centuries she had grown used to the old size of the command center, having the chairmen's chairs down on the lower level in front of the big screen, then a half-circle of stations behind her, up two steps, then another half-circle of stations around the back wall, up two more steps.

It made the big room feel like a college amphitheater she had classes in back at the University of Oregon. The room was big and impressive, sure, yet small enough that the entire command crew could work as a team.

After they had finished the war with the aliens, which had taken them over three hundred years on the original *Star Fall*, Chairman Ray and Chairman Tacita, the founders of the Seeders, had asked her and Matt if they would be interested in having *Star Fall* shifted to a new and much larger ship for an exploration mission.

A mission that might take them a thousand years to complete. But a critical one to make sure the human galaxies were never threatened again as they had been with the alien infestation.

Both she and Matt, her co-chairman and partner for life, had agreed, and when *Star Fall* agreed to move to the newer, bigger ship, everything had been set.

The construction of the new ship had taken almost twenty years. And now, at fifty years into the new mission, Carey still enjoyed the challenge of every day.

She couldn't imagine ever getting tired of it, actually.

They were going to explore beyond the edge of known space.

She was halfway finished with the morning's reports from the thousand scout ships they had out at the moment when Matt appeared at her side. He was sweating and had just come from doing five miles on one of the many tracks on *Star Fall*.

She didn't even glance at the handsome man she was more in love with now than the day she met him. She knew he would be sweaty and his short brown hair would be going in all directions. It seemed to always do that, even when he tried to comb it.

"Don't even think about hugging me," she said without looking away from the reports scanning past on the big screen.

"Would never think of it," he said, laughing.

A couple of other command crew behind them chuckled. It was almost a standing joke that he would show up after exercise in the command center and try to give her a sweaty hug.

"You know you and your team don't stand a chance this year," he said.

She turned and looked at his sweating face and his grin. "Seems to me that your team has lost to my team every year now for six years."

"Seven," one of the command crew said.

"Seven," she said, smiling.

"This is our year," he said, frowning past her at whoever had corrected her.

"I think this year you should just work on finishing," she said, glancing back up at the screen and all the reports, trying not to smile.

He snorted and said nothing. The last two years his teams hadn't even finished the Tip-to-Tip race, although she had to admit they had given it a good try both years.

The Tip-to-Tip race had been Matt's brainchild about twenty years into the new mission. The new *Star Fall* was so massive, holding over three million people, that Matt had thought it would be fun to have a relay race with ten member teams starting at the bow of the ship and running through the entire ship to the stern, then back to the front.

Tip-to-Tip was born.

It wasn't until the two of them, in their apartment one night, working with *Star Fall*, had discovered just how far that race would be.

Both she and Matt were from an Earth with a country called the United States. The length of the new *Star Fall* was from coast-to-coast. Two-thousand, eight-hundred miles from the front to the back of the ship, about four-thousand, five hundred kilometers.

So Tip-to-Tip would be over nine-thousand kilometers. Or about nine-hundred ten-kilometer races, all linked.

Without a break.

Last year the winning team had done the relay race in just under thirty-eight days. Each member had to run or walk ten kilometers before passing the monitored armband to the next team member.

There were ship hangars on *Star Fall* that were larger than some of the old states in the United States. The ship had been built in space to explore for a thousand years with three million men, women, and children. The ship had been built to go beyond any known space and explore along the way as it went.

It was long, shaped in ways like a long bird, and was the size of a decent moon. Its shields were so powerful that on trans-tunnel drive it could plow through a planet and not even notice it had hit something.

So at first, because of the size of *Star Fall*, Matt's idea of a Tip-to-Tip relay race seemed impossible. But the more they thought about it, the more fun it sounded and now it was a major yearly event for the ship.

Also, it would give a lot of the people living on *Star Fall* some reason to exercise.

Last year over eight-hundred teams had signed up. And Carey had to admit the race was grueling and a lot more fun than she had ever imagined it to be.

This year's Tip-to-Tip race started in ten days. And she and her team were ready. They wouldn't win it, but all that mattered to her was beating Matt's team.

Bragging rights for a full year were wonderful.

TWO

AFTER HIS WORKOUT, Chairman Matt Ladel climbed out of the shower, finished dressing in his normal dress shirt, jeans, and tennis shoes, and then checked in with the other nine members of his relay team. All of them were feeling healthy and ready to go.

And so was he. And in three team meetings over the last few months, they had a pretty good plan worked out on how they were going to run the race this year. And barring injuries that had happened the last two years, they would make it.

Last year four of the ten of them had been forced to drop out around day twenty. Running a ten-kilometer leg every ten hours could really stress the body. And most teams didn't finish with all ten of their members still running.

But when they lost four team members, Matt and the others found it almost

impossible to run a ten-kilometer leg every six hours. They managed to give it a try, but after three more days, they finally had tossed it in.

Matt couldn't remember being that sore or that tired before.

They had still been in the top three hundred teams, since most teams every year drop out much sooner. Last year only one-hundred-and-forty of the eight-hundred-plus teams that started actually finished.

Carey's team had been one of the finishers and he hadn't heard the end of it all year.

He was in their apartment kitchen, working on getting himself a small snack of cheese and crackers when Carey paged him from the command center.

"Matt. Got an issue."

He knew that tone and those words. When Carey said they had an issue, it wasn't something he waited around for.

He popped a piece of cheese in his mouth and jumped to her side in the command center. Every Seeder could teleport, the only way it was possible to get around on a ship this size.

"We have a scout ship missing," she said as he appeared beside her. "*The Bee.*"

He studied the report on the big screen in front of their chair. He knew the chairman of *The Bee*. Chairman Reed, a good man, an experienced chairman.

Reed liked to smile a lot and drink his beer on off hours. For a Seeder, he was stout and solid. In fact, he was known as a superb brewer and a number of the pubs he liked served his beer at times.

The Bee carried almost two thousand in crew and families and was on a standard one-week mission with a small military ship shadowing it.

All scout ships went out on rotation for one week, then returned for three weeks so the families and such could have some stability on *Star Fall*. In fact, most families stayed home instead of going along on the week-long missions, even though every person or family on a scout ship had a home both on the scout ship and on *Star Fall*.

The mission of a scout ship was to jump ahead of *Star Fall* and scout galaxies along the route for any signs of alien life.

Seeders had discovered that the universe was mostly empty. Only two races had ever developed the technology to go between galaxies. Humans and the Gray, and the Gray had been first.

Seeders were the branch of humanity that lived a long time and seeded human culture in new galaxies. The aliens they had had to fight were a runaway human experiment.

So the mission Matt and Carey and *Star Fall* was on now was to explore outward beyond the edge of the known universe in search of other advanced civilizations, if any existed.

There were now fourteen ships the size of *Star Fall* moving outward in a starburst pattern, exploring. So far, no ship had come across anything more than a few emerging alien races in a galaxy. And sadly, most of those races would never develop far enough to get off their home planet, let alone survive long enough to expand out into their own galaxy.

But Seeders stayed away from even those low-level alien civilizations, making note of them and then never entering the galaxy again. Space was big enough and empty enough to not need to.

Sometimes Matt found it stunning the scale Seeders worked at. The speeds of the scout ships and of *Star Fall* were such that entire galaxies with billions of stars could go past like signposts on a road.

And right now *Star Fall* was only at half speed, allowing the scout ships to fan out in all directions, scan entire galaxies and report back in. Over a thousand scout ships were out at any given time.

But in fifty years now of this mission, they had not had a scout ship go missing.

Matt didn't like the feeling of this at all.

THREE

CAREY GLANCED AT Matt when he appeared beside her. She let him get his bearings and see the problem, then the two of them moved to their command chairs.

The two chairs were molded together and when in the chairs the two of them could almost be a part of *Star Fall* and absorb so much more data.

Matt took her hand and they sat down. They always held hands when in the chair. It allowed them to feel more in contact with each other as well as *Star Fall*.

The chair formed in around them, a familiar feeling that Carey had grown to love over the centuries.

"Star Fall, show us the last images coming in from *The Bee,"* Carey said.

In front of their eyes the image appeared as if they were looking at an approaching galaxy from the perspective of *The Bee*. It seemed like a normal spiral galaxy, small, but nothing unusual. And it had no reading coming from it.

The Bee planned on holding just at the edge and scanning, then if finding no immediate signs of civilization, doing a complete circuit of the outer edge of the galaxy, then if still clear, *The Bee* would make a pass through the galaxy before moving on to the next galaxy in their week-long mission.

Everything looked perfectly normal until suddenly all data and the image simply cut off.

"Star Fall," Matt said, "any sign of failure on *The Bee* in any way."

"No," Star Fall said. *"Up until the instant of cut-off, all systems were functioning in normal ranges."*

"Theories?" Carey asked.

"I have no explanation for this occurrence," Star Fall said.

Carey did not like the sound of that in the slightest.

"Empty space bubble they missed?" Matt asked.

Carey nodded. That would account for such a sudden vanishing, but all empty space bubbles were tracked by all ships carefully and the Seeders had actually used empty space bubbles as a weapon in the war against the aliens.

"No," Star Fall said simply.

Matt glanced at Carey and she turned slightly to look at him. She could tell he was worried, more worried than she had seen him since the early days of the war.

"I assume the military escort ship with *The Bee* recorded the same thing?" Matt asked.

The military escort ship was the *Sinclair*, with Commander Tulo in charge. Every scout ship had a much smaller military ship shadowing it, usually screened.

"It did," Star Fall said. *"Commander Tulo reported the missing ship the moment it happened and took up a standby position near where* The Bee *vanished."*

"We need to stop and bring in all scout ships," Matt said.

Carey nodded. "I agree. And then send a dozen more scout ships with military escorts to surround the galaxy, but not approach."

"Agreed," Matt said.

They both stood.

Carey turned to the command crew, many of them she had worked with for centuries. Worry covered all their faces.

"We're going to a full stop and bring in all scout ships," Carey said.

No one said a word. A couple of them nodded.

Beside her Matt said, *"Star Fall, please drop out of trans-tunnel flight."*

"Emergency recall all scout ships," Carey said. "Including *The Bee*. See if they can hear us and we just can't see or hear them."

Carey turned with Matt to watch the main board as the thousand plus scout ships and their military escorts responded to the return call.

Two minutes later all had responded but *The Bee*.

Carey felt her stomach twisting in a knot.

"How long until all ships are back on board?" Matt asked a fraction of a second before Carey could.

"Three hours," Star Fall said.

Carey turned to Matt. "We need to get this ship and the scout ships returning protected."

Matt nodded.

"Star Fall," he said, "tell the second and the fifth military units to launch on emergency status and protect all returning scout ships and this ship against any threat."

Carey knew that would launch over two hundred high-powered military ships with defensive and offensive capabilities. No families on the military ships.

Star Fall had the capabilities of full defense and offense as well, but no point in taking any chances at all with the three million lives that were on board.

Of the three million souls on board *Star Fall*, over eight hundred thousand were military and their families. For thousands of years, Seeders had not really needed a military branch. But since the war it had become a regular part of any Seeder mission and Carey was very glad they had the military with them now.

FOUR

THREE HOURS LATER Matt felt a giant sigh of relief as the last of the scout ships and small military escort ships were back on *Star Fall*. In the three hours, ten of the larger scout ships, without families on board, had launched with ten of the full battle cruisers as escorts, all headed for the galaxy where *The Bee* had vanished.

Matt knew they might be overreacting on all of this, but when two thousand of his people suddenly went missing, he didn't want to take any chances with any others.

As he and Carey watched on the big screen, the twenty ships arrived near the galaxy where *The Bee* had vanished and spread out, keeping their distance, but moving quickly to surround the entire small spiral galaxy.

The galaxy was just over a hundred-thousand light-years across and had just over three hundred billion stars in it. Smaller than their home Milky Way Galaxy. From all the scans coming in, there was nothing at all special about this small spiral galaxy, and no signs of life at all.

But Matt had a gut sense this small place was very, very special.

Eight of the scout ships with their military escorts took up positions at points around the outside of the galaxy and one ship went above and another below the galaxy core.

"Anything unusual?" Carey asked *Star Fall* as the scans from all of the scout ships came in.

"Nothing is beyond any standard parameter," *Star Fall* said.

Suddenly Matt had an idea that seemed so stupid to him, he almost decided to not say it, but then went ahead.

"Have each scout ship scan for the scout ship directly across from them through the galaxy."

Carey looked at him, frowning, then turned back to the big screen to watch the data flowing in.

"Some field is blocking the scans through the galaxy," *Star Fall* said.

Matt nodded, trying to make himself take a deep breath. That was exactly what he had been afraid of.

"Are you kidding me?" Carey said. "That galaxy is just a massive image hiding something else?"

Matt nodded. They had to get those ships away from whatever that was.

"Star Fall, pull all ships back from that galaxy. Emergency."

On the screen all ships moved at once, moving away from galaxy at full trans-tunnel drive.

Twenty minutes later they were back on board and the number of military ships launched and protecting *Star Fall* had increased by fifty.

"Now what?" Carey asked, turning to look at him.

"We stay here and gather data, as much as we can from this distance, then we call for help."

Carey nodded. "You think Chairman Ray and Chairman Tacita might know what is going on here?"

"Since they have been known to keep things from us in the past, nothing would surprise me," Matt said.

What he didn't say was that he had a hunch this vast mission of sending ships out to explore the known universe had some smaller goals in mind as well. And chances are they had just found one of those goals.

But Carey clearly had been following his thinking.

"Star Fall," Carey said, "please put up a three-dimensional image of the area around the original Earth galaxy. And show in green all human space."

The big screen filled completely with white dots, each tiny dot representing an entire galaxy. One area spreading to the right was green dots. Matt had seen this image before and found it amazing that all those millions of galaxies were filled with humans thanks to the work of the Seeders.

"Now," Carey said, "please reduce the scale enough that shows the original Earth galaxy, the human space, and our location at the moment."

The green human space became a tiny green line to one side of the large screen with the original Earth galaxy near one end of the line. Matt found it stunning that they had traveled so far in only fifty years.

"I don't think this is from old Earth," Matt said, knowing what Carey was hoping.

Carey nodded. *"Star Fall,* with the old standard trans-tunnel drive, how long would it have taken a ship to get from the original Earth to this point?"

Star Fall said simply, *"Original Earth would not have yet been formed as a planet at the point the ship would have needed to start."*

Matt could tell that deflated Carey completely.

"So we are dealing with something alien, clearly," Matt said. "Or something natural we don't understand."

Carey nodded. "We need help."

"That we do," Matt said. "That we do. But first we need more information."

FIVE

CAREY JUST KEPT studying the image of the small spiral galaxy as the next day went by. No sign of *The Bee* which scared her more than she wanted to admit, and no data at all other than the fact that any probe they sent into the galaxy from any direction simply vanished.

They actually had no idea at all what had caused the probes and *The Bee* to vanish. There was just nothing there to even take readings on.

Carey and Matt both thought that the entire thing seemed to be acting like the skin of an empty-space bubble. With an empty-space bubble, all time and energy inside the bubble didn't exist. The bubbles were formed by forces in space that caused areas of space to be devoid of time. You couldn't see the boundary of an empty-space bubble, but you could go through the edge of one and just vanish as *The Bee* had done, and the probes had done.

But the largest empty-space bubble possible with the math they knew was just over a hundred light-years across, and was round, not the oblong shape of a hundred-thousand light-year spiral galaxy.

Plus Seeders knew how to spot and avoid empty-space bubbles. This was not one of them, *Star Fall* assured them.

Finally, on the morning of the second day of doing experiments, Carey glanced at Matt. "I think it's time we call in some help."

Neither one of them had left the command center except to eat and shower. And Carey was exhausted. They had had periods like this in the war, but she had hoped these kinds of emergencies had been behind them.

Matt nodded. "*Star Fall*, please send word to *Star Mist* and *Star Rain* that an emergency chairman meeting is needed. Also include Chairman Ray and Chairman Tacita."

"*Message sent,*" *Star Fall* said.

Carey knew there was no way she or Matt or any of the other chairmen could teleport from such a vast distance. And also, each ship as it went out on the mission had left what they called "Breadcrumbs" behind it.

Carey and Matt, as chairmen, had the ability to teleport millions of light years, but most Seeders on *Star Fall* could only teleport about one-hundred-thousand light years at a time. So on *Star Fall* was an entire factory producing small self-sustaining stations with beacons. Each station could hold upwards of a hundred people at a time, with bedrooms, kitchens, and other things to make someone comfortable.

The stations were placed as they went along every hundred-thousand light years. So anyone who wanted to go back to their home galaxy in the human occupied space could do so at any point, jumping from station to station. It might take them a month or so of jumps and resting to go back, but the path was available which gave everyone on *Star Fall* the feeling of still being attached to their home worlds in human space.

Every few hundred stations there was a major station, with full-time staff and crew that could hold upwards of five thousand residents if necessary. Carey thought of them as huge resort hotels just floating in space. And they were as opulent as resorts, with lavish pools and spas and restaurants. Plus some of the best traveling entertainment played the station circuit.

With fourteen large ships like *Star Fall* headed out, the major stations were expanding their numbers all the time. And it had become a large industry to staff those stations if nothing more than Seeders wanting to jump into deep space for dinner and a night's entertainment.

So far, in fifty years, they had planted over one thousand stations, with ten major resort-like stations. And members of the crew moved along the path regularly, often jumping back just to take in a special band or act from human space.

Carey was just constantly amazed at the scale Seeders just took for granted. She supposed that once you worked on seeding an entire galaxy and billions of planets with humans and helping each civilization grow and expand safely, jumping through space seemed pretty simple.

"All have answered," Star Fall said. *"Chairman Ray and Tacita have their ship docked near factories in the Milky Way. They suggested you all meet there in ten minutes."*

"Tell them we agree," Carey said as Matt nodded.

He took her hand and a moment later they had jumped to the large resort of *Angel*, the fifth resort they had launched along the trail of crumbs. They had launched *Angel* over thirty years ago and it had become a popular vacation spot, being added onto over the decades because of a fantastic image of a giant nebula nearby called Angel.

From what Carey understood, *Angel* now had a permanent population of fifty thousand and could hold ten times that many people.

They had appeared near the Lagoon Bar and Restaurant and went to the bar to get some iced tea.

The Lagoon Bar sat on the edge of a large lake, surrounded by all sorts of tropical plants and trees. A few hundred people were scattered around the many tables, all drinking and laughing. Above them the ceiling was open to a large clear force field bubble showing a fantastic view of the reds and greens and oranges of the nearby Angel Nebula.

"Chairmen," Johnny Bens said as they approached. "It's been far too long."

Johnny Bens ran the Lagoon and was as nice a man as Carey had met. He never seemed to not have a smile on his face and a nice thing to say.

"Headed for a meeting," Carey said after giving Johnny a kiss over the bar. "Need a couple of those wonderful iced teas of yours."

"My pleasure," Johnny said, setting to work to build them. "So when are you two going to come back for some dancing and drinks and dinner, on me?"

"Soon, we hope," Matt said.

"Very soon," Carey said. "But first we have a few things to take care of and then in a week my team and I have to beat him again in the Tip-to-Tip."

Johnny just laughed. "I hear that crazy race of yours has now spread to all fourteen Starburst ships. And there is talk here about sending a few teams from *Angel* to compete."

Carey just laughed at that. "The more the merrier."

Johnny just shook his head and laughed. "I think they are crazy."

After they had both tasted their iced teas, thanked Johnny and promised to return soon, Matt once again took her hand and a moment later they were back in their home galaxy, standing in a stark, old-feeling meeting room with a large wood table and leather chairs.

"You would think after this many centuries they would change the look of this place," Matt said, glancing around.

Carey had to admit, it looked exactly the same as it had when she and Matt had first been recruited to become Seeders. This room had scared her to death.

Now it just looked old and dated.

She and Matt took their normal positions at the big table. She didn't like being here at all. They hadn't had a meeting here since before the Starburst program started.

It didn't feel good now to be back.

SIX

ANGIE AND GAGE from *Star Mist* were the next to arrive, followed by Benny and Gina from *Star Rain*.

Matt was stunned at how excited he was to see his four friends. It had been the six of them that had been recruited because they were new and fresh and could fight the aliens' infestation.

And all of them had decided to take their ships into the Starburst program.

All four of them looked the same as they had fifty years before and three hundred years before that. None of them aged or changed how they dressed.

Just as Matt and Carey stayed in jeans and informal shirts and blouses, so did the other four. Just as Matt did, Benny kept the sleeves of his dress shirt rolled up, but unlike Matt, Benny kept his dark hair cut military short. Both Benny and Gina were tall and both were in perfect shape. Gina kept her long black hair pulled back and tied.

Angie also had long black hair that she kept pulled back and Gage looked more like a fashion model than anything else, with intense dark eyes and a short military haircut that looked stylish on him.

Matt couldn't believe how much he missed being around them. Once they got this problem solved that brought them here, he needed to suggest the six of them get together regularly, even if they were farther apart in space than any human could imagine.

After a few minutes of catching up and laughing, Chairmen Ray and Tacita showed up. They were two of the oldest Seeders still alive at millions of years old. Matt had no idea, even after living for going on four hundred years now, how anyone could live that long. But they had.

Both were tall and stately looking. Ray looked to be middle-aged with long bright silver hair that reached down his back. Tacita had short, shining black hair that gave her a stern look. As far as Matt was concerned, it matched her personality.

They were the ones that had come up with the Starburst program to send out exploring ships to make sure no surprise threatened human space.

When they sat down at the table with a smile at everyone, the rest of them sat as well.

"It is good to have this team back together again," Ray said. "But I am in the dark as to why?"

Matt nodded, glanced at Carey who indicated he should tell them what happened.

"We have a missing scout ship," Matt said. "Chairman Ray, could you have your ship put me in contact with *Star Fall?*"

"You are now," Ray said.

"Star Fall, would you please transmit the image of *The Bee* going missing, from the military escort *Sinclair's* vantage point."

A moment later the image of *The Bee* moving through space toward the spiral galaxy came into being in the middle of the table. For ten seconds nothing seemed to happen, then suddenly *The Bee* vanished.

"Empty space bubble?" Gage asked.

"No," Carey said. "But taking tests, we discovered that something is not allowing scans to pass through the galaxy. We had scout ships on both sides of the galaxy trying to scan each other, but all signals were being blocked."

The image of the spiral galaxy vanished, leaving the room quiet.

"We are at full stop and all scout ships have returned to *Star Fall,*" Matt said. "We have half our military launched and surrounding *Star Fall* until we discover what this might be."

"Are you saying that galaxy is completely surrounded by a shield of some sort?" Gage asked.

Carey was watching Ray and Tacita as Matt said, "Yes, that is exactly what we are saying. And we know it can't be human caused because at the old trans-tunnel speeds, no ship could have gone that far."

Ray and Tacita both just frowned.

"Natural event of some sort or another?" Angie asked.

"We honestly don't know," Carey said. "But it feels artificial to all of us."

"So why would an entire galaxy be shielded?" Tacita asked.

Matt shrugged. Carey said nothing.

Finally it was Benny who said simply, "Because something inside that galaxy doesn't want to be found."

"But as empty as space is," Gina asked, "Why?"

Carey suddenly got shivers up and down her back. She glanced at Matt who clearly was thinking the same thing from how his face had gone white.

"Because maybe there's something ahead of us," Carey said. "Or to the side

of us. Something that scares hell out of whatever is inside that shield."

Silence once again filled the meeting room. And with the eight of them, Carey knew that wasn't a good sign.

SEVEN

FOR THE NEXT hour the eight of them kicked around every idea they could think of. Nothing made sense.

Matt hated that not a one of them could even come close to an idea.

So they decided to work down in the details first. They all agreed to change the protocols of a scout ship approaching a galaxy on all fourteen of the Starburst ships. The scout ship and military escort was to stand off first and send in a probe. That would have saved *The Bee* from being trapped in whatever it was trapped in.

They also decided that all fourteen Starburst ships and their scientists should work on this problem, so *Star Fall* would send them all every bit of data that came in.

Also, Ray would contact the experts on empty space bubbles and see if they had come up with a way to seeing inside an empty space bubble. That kind of technology might work on this shield, or whatever it was.

And Ray would get every scientist he thought might have a chance of solving what that shield was looking at it.

And in the meantime, *Star Fall* would send a thousand scout ships ahead of its location, all escorted by military, and all shielded, to see what was ahead.

That protocol would also be changed for all Starburst ships. Until now they hadn't been scouting that far ahead. That was to change for all of them now.

Ray and Tacita left first, then after hugs all around, Matt took Carey's hand and with only a short pause at Angel Station, they were back on *Star Fall*.

"Any changes?" Carey asked as they appeared in the command center.

Matt hadn't expected there to be and there wasn't.

So over the next few minutes they worked with the command crew to get five hundred scout ships headed forward, another three hundred headed to the left of the shielded galaxy at a ninety-degree angle of *Star Fall's* path and another three hundred headed to the right at a ninety-degree angle.

They were all to spread out and cover as many galaxies and space as they could. And they all had orders to stay shielded.

Matt didn't much like the idea that whatever was in the galaxy was hiding from something. But they needed to find out for sure if that was a possibility. If it was, and some form of alien race had gone to the extreme measure of hiding from something, Matt didn't like the idea of drawing that something's attention to humanity.

But at this point, the Starburst program was designed to discover things like this. He just didn't want to lose two thousand good people on *The Bee* in the process.

In three hundred years of war with the aliens, they hadn't lost a ship or a person. Now was not the time to start. But the alien war had been different because the aliens were different. They didn't even know they were in a war.

The aliens, as they called them, were a runaway genetics experiment done by a distant branch of humans from the original Earth. They thought they could make a lower-level rat-like race intelligent, so they had basically genetically enhanced them enough to be able to construct space ships and get to other planets and galaxies. But at their very core they were still rats with the focus to expand and breed.

Within seven hundred years they could completely expand over an entire galaxy. They would just keep breeding and building starships until they depleted a planet. Then because the planet couldn't support them, they would turn on each other and eventually die out. But not until they had sent millions of ships per planet to new planets and new galaxies.

The Seeders had decided to just stop the ships from expanding to other planets and leave them alone on the planets. Matt knew that they had been lucky to stop the aliens because all it took was one alien ship before the infestation started all over.

After two hours, Matt suggested to Carey that they go to their apartment and he cook them dinner. She had agreed and they had jumped there.

Their apartment suited the two of them. They had decorated it in brown and wood tones, with lots of images of Earth on the walls to give them a sense of windows.

Their master bedroom was huge, with two walk-in closets, a high ceiling with wood beams, and a massive bed with quilts on it because they both liked to sleep cold.

Their living room had what appeared to be a real stone fireplace and comfortable brown-cloth couches. One entire wall was full of books. Around the room books and reading tablets scattered over the coffee table and end tables. Matt loved that it was contained cluttered with reading material. It felt like home.

A large screen on one wall allowed them to watch movies and Matt made the best popcorn ever, he was convinced, with just enough butter and salt to make it impossible to stop eating while watching a movie.

The large dining area and kitchen was where they spent the most time however. The kitchen was perfect, with lots of counter space to prepare anything either one of them wanted to cook. And it had every imaginable kitchen help appliance.

And the dining table right near the kitchen could sit eight people easily.

Carey dropped into a chair at the dining table while Matt poured her a glass of fruit juice and another glass of water. Then he went back to start working on a fresh salad to go with the cold chicken they still had left over from last night.

"Are you scared by all this?" Carey asked after a moment.

"Totally," Matt said. "And I'm really scared for all those people on *The Bee.*"

"What do you think happened to them?" she asked.

"Honestly," he said, glancing up for a moment before going back to work on chopping some onions for the salad, "I am hoping that Reed realized they had passed through something, or into something they hadn't expected, and immediately cloaked."

"He can think that quick," Carey said, nodding, "no doubt there."

"Even though we move around galaxies like they are dots on a map," Matt said, chopping up some lettuce, "galaxies are actually huge places, so if he got inside some barrier he couldn't get out of, he might also be able to hide from whatever built the barrier."

"So lots of positive outcomes," Carey said.

Matt could only nod to that because there was no reason at all to talk about the negative outcomes. He knew they both thought about them enough.

"So what do we do now?" Carey asked as Matt finished tossing the salad and put it in a bowl.

"Besides eat dinner," he said, "we wait and study and research and explore until we have answers."

She nodded, glancing at the salad as he put a plate of cold chicken in front of her and then plates and silverware in front of both of them.

"We have all of the Starburst ships and their scientists on the task," Matt said, "plus all the top Seeder scientists in human space. Someone will find an answer."

"And what happens if we don't?" Carey asked.

"Humanity and Seeders never go without an answer for long," Matt said, dishing up his salad. "That's in our nature."

Carey said nothing to that and they ate in silence, both worrying and thinking.

SECTION TWO
Discovery

EIGHT

IT WAS THE next morning, after a long and sleepless night, that they started to learn something about the area of space they had stumbled into.

Ahead on their planned course, scout ships found six more shielded galaxies. That stunned Carey, and worried her even more. Some race, or some entity, had enough knowledge and desire to shield an entire galaxy, make it look just like any other empty galaxy in the area of space.

And that meant, without a doubt, they were dealing with a race or an entity that could travel between galaxies. And except for the Gray and humans, no race had ever been found that had managed that.

"Stay shielded and stay back and just observe," Matt had told each scout ship near a shielded galaxy.

"You think whoever is doing that knows we are out here?" Carey asked.

Matt shrugged. "We would know if alien ships came into human space, so I'm betting we are known. Especially if whatever or whoever is behind those shields are hiding."

Carey flat hated that thought. And for the first time in fifty years started to doubt the idea of the Starburst program. All was fine as long as the universe stayed mostly empty, but this became a different problem when they suddenly found themselves trespassing into other's known space.

"Star Fall," Matt said. "Show this area of space on the big screen and color all shielded galaxies in red."

"And add in as green dots all our scout ships and their locations," Carey said.

On the big wall-sized board the image appeared. It showed about eight thousand or so galaxies. The location of the *Star Fall* was a large green dot, the shielded galaxies were directly ahead of their path.

As they were staring at the image, another galaxy white dot turned red. And then within moments another.

And then another as scout ships reported in their findings.

Carey just stared, her mouth open. If this was a civilization, they were staring at a massive one.

But why shield every galaxy and what kind of technology and energy would it take to do such a task over and over?

It was Matt who saw the pattern. "The galaxies are all in a line."

The moment Matt said that Carey could see it as well. And behind them one of the command crew said softly, "I'll be."

Another said, "Bread crumbs."

Carey knew exactly what they meant. This looked, at galaxy size, exactly like what they had been doing with their jump stations back to human space. Many galaxies beside the ones with shields were normal, no shields, no signs of civilization-level life at all.

"They are pretty much the same distance apart as well," Matt said.

Carey didn't like the way she was thinking, but she had to tell Matt. "These could be like our Bread Crumb stations, but these also could form a wall. Posts in a defensive or offensive wall."

Matt just shook his head. "And I thought Seeders worked at a massive scale. We're playing with toys compared to this level."

Over the next two hours they had the scout ships target certain galaxies ahead they thought would be shielded and every one turned out to be. And they sent a hundred scout ships along the line of shielded galaxies going back, since none of the likely ones had been scouted as they came by. They had been too far off *Star Fall's* main course.

And they found more.

Finally, when they had over sixty shielded galaxies, Carey asked *Star Fall,* "Is there a pattern to what we are finding in shielded galaxies? Can you extrapolate out any kind of findings from the data we have now?"

"*Yes,*" *Star Fall* said, surprising Carey and clearly Matt.

"What would that be?" Matt asked.

"*If this pattern were to continue, the shielded galaxies form a circle,*" *Star Fall* said.

Carey just stared at the images of the shielded galaxy.

"A two-dimensional circle or a sphere?" Matt asked after a moment.

"*Not enough data,*" *Star Fall* said.

"Please indicate the galaxies, following this pattern, that would show both a circle and a sphere?" Carey said. "Increase the image to show the area of either the circle or the sphere and include human space."

The entire wall seemed to turn white again with more dots representing galaxies than Carey could ever imagine. Human space was again shown as a small almost river of green along one side. The alien circle was shown in red and the possible sphere was shown in pink.

It was so massive Carey couldn't even begin to grasp it. It covered more billions of galaxies and all of human space was tiny compared to the size, if this thing actually existed.

"*Star Fall,*" Matt said, "will any of the other Starburst ships come close to this sphere or circle?"

"*Yes,*" *Star Fall* said, "*Star Rain crosses into this circle or sphere in one year at their present half speed.*"

A line appeared on the large screen coming from human space showing the path of *Star Rain.*

"Well," Matt said, "we can find out just how big this thing really is in short order."

"Are we sure we want to know?" Carey asked.

Matt shrugged. "This is what we are out here to find, isn't it?"

Carey just shook her head. Not in her wildest imagination, even after being in space for over three hundred years, could she have imagined something like this.

NINE

FOR THE NEXT two days, all Matt and Carey did was look at reports from scout ships coming in. And worry and try to figure out a way to get *The Bee* out from behind that shield.

And it had taken at top speed a number of scout ships from *Star Rain* to get to where the edge of the circle or sphere might be to explore it from that side, if indeed it did actually exist. Those reports were about to come in.

But after the last two days, Matt was convinced what they were seeing was a massive sphere made up of millions and millions of shielded galaxies around the edge and containing more billions of galaxies inside the sphere. He was sure that *Star Fall* had the exact number of galaxies contained inside the sphere, but so far he hadn't wanted to ask.

Yesterday, Carey had sent out military escorted science ships to study any kind of connection that might be happening between shielded galaxies. There had to be a reason for such a massive undertaking, but Matt had a hunch that Seeders were so primitive compared to the race that built these galaxy shields, they might not be able to understand it.

Not once, but numbers of times both he and Carey had mentioned they felt like ants on a human's pant leg.

"*Report coming in from Star Rain,*" *Star Fall* said.

On the big screen the image of space showing the possible sphere five red dots

lined up near where *Star Rain's* scout ships had gone.

"The scout ships have found five shielded galaxies," Star Fall said. *"There is now a very high percentage the shielded galaxies forms a complete sphere."*

Matt just stared at the sphere illustrated on the large screen, trying to make any kind of sense of what he was staring at. It just completely baffled him.

Why?

Carey kept staring at the large sphere, then she asked a question that he hadn't thought to ask.

"Star Fall, what is at the center of this sphere? Can you show an image of the galaxies in the center?"

"No," Star Fall said. *"There are no galaxies anywhere near the center of this sphere that can be detected."*

"Empty space?" Matt asked.

"Undetermined," Star Fall said. *"And the scout ship* The Bee *has reappeared."*

Matt coughed and then stared at Carey.

A stunned silence filled the command center.

"Please contact Chairman Reed," Carey said before Matt could.

"He is contacting you," Star Fall said.

"On the big screen," Matt said.

A moment later the smiling and clearly healthy face of Chairman Reed appeared.

"Great to see you again," Matt said.

"Great to be seen, Chairmen," Reed said, smiling and bowing slightly. "Seems I got myself and my ship into a little pickle."

"We noticed," Carey said, laughing. "But wait until you find out what your little adventure uncovered. Is everyone on your ship all right? No damages or injuries."

"No damages or injuries beyond an entire crew being scared out of our minds," Reed said. "Every detail will be in all our reports, but if you would like,

I can summarize what we found on the other side of that shield."

"Please," Carey said, again a half second before Matt could say the same thing.

"Inside that shield the rest of the universe vanished," Reed said. "So we instantly knew we had gone through something and we cloaked."

Matt nodded. He had hoped that would be the case.

"From the inside," Reed said, "the shield looks like a shimmering surface of a lake surrounding the entire galaxy. Only it was an oblong, like we were inside a strangely shaped ball. Never saw anything like it. Think of looking at a surface of shimmering mercury."

"Could you spot the power source?" Matt asked.

"There was none that we could find," Reed said. "And we spent a lot of our time trying to figure out if we would be destroyed going back through the shield. That is what took us so long to come back out."

Matt nodded. Logical thinking and if he had been in charge of *The Bee*, he would have done exactly the same thing that Reed had done and just as carefully.

No power source at all?" Carey asked.

"None that we could locate," Reed said. "We think it might be a natural form."

"It's not," Matt said. "You'll understand when you get the rest of what we have discovered while you were in there."

"Any signs of civilization?" Carey asked.

"Yes," Reed said. "At one point in the distant history of the galaxy, a fairly advanced civilization traveled among the stars of the galaxy inside the sphere. But the best that we could figure with limited time to study what we could find, that civilization died out almost a million years ago. No idea why."

"So going through the shield caused no problems to anyone or your ship?" Matt asked. If that was the case they could go back in and study.

"None," Reed said. "We tested and retested everything we could, but we could never get a reading on what the shield even was. So we voted. I figured all of our lives were at stake, so everyone needed a vote. The entire adult crew voted one-hundred-percent to take a chance and go back through."

"Well come on in and we'll talk some more," Matt said. "Get your crew settled and all reports filed so *Star Fall* can put it all together."

"Glad to," Reed said.

"And Chairman," Carey said. "Great job."

"Thank you," Reed said, smiling.

With that the screen went blank.

Matt exhaled. He hadn't realized how much tension he had been holding with every hour that ship and all the people on board were missing.

Now Available
from all your favorite booksellers in trade paper and electronic editions.

Behind them the command crew were all cheering and laughing. It seemed they had all felt the same stress.

"Star Fall," Matt said. "Please inform the other Starburst ships and Chairmen Ray and Tacita that our lost scout ship has returned intact and they will be getting data shortly."

"Done," Star Fall said.

Matt nodded and turned to the smiling faces of their command crew. "Now, everyone, we need some ideas on how to explore this giant sphere we have stumbled across. After lunch, Carey and I will be willing to listen to anything, no matter how wild."

"From the looks of the size of the sphere," Carey said, "the wilder the better."

With that, Matt jumped them both back to their apartment where he needed desperately to just hug Carey.

And it seemed she had needed to hug him back.

TEN

TWO DAYS LATER they had a plan. They were headed to the center of the sphere.

Carey wasn't completely sure she liked that idea, but they just couldn't keep on going as if they had never found this fantastic alien construction. They needed answers.

Also, Benny and Gina with *Star Rain* were going to leave their path and also head for the center of the sphere. With two of the Starburst ships and all the thousands of military and scout and science ships with each Starburst ship, the chairmen of all the Starburst ships figured there was a chance of discovering what this sphere was all about.

Plus, honestly, Carey felt much better having *Star Rain* and its major fleet of ships as backup to them. There was no telling what they might find with a civilization that could build with such massive reach.

Both *Star Fall* and *Star Rain* were going to travel at half speed, just as they had been doing, to allow scout ships to explore everything around them and ahead of them. At that speed, it would take them four or five years each to reach the center of the sphere.

Maybe by the time they got there, they would know what was happening and who had built the sphere of shielded galaxies.

Carey was working on breakfast on the morning of the eleventh day after *The Bee* returned when the command center paged her and Matt.

"Chairmen, you are needed in command."

Carey grabbed her orange juice, made sure no heat was left on and went down the hall. Matt was in the shower.

"Call from command," she said.

"Shit," he said, and the water turned off.

"Meet you there."

With that, she jumped to a spot beside their command chairs.

"Chairman," Gina said, smiling from the large screen in front of Carey. Benny stood beside her. Both looked very serious.

Matt will be here in a moment," Carey said.

At that moment Matt appeared, his hair still wet and his shirt unbuttoned. But he had at least managed to get on his jeans and slippers. He was working to button the shirt.

"Sorry for the early morning interruption," Benny said, "but we figure you two would want to know what our two ships have discovered."

Carey nodded. "*Star Fall*, please explain."

She wasn't liking the sound of this at all.

Star Fall said, *"We have managed to combine our resources to get an image of what is at the center of the sphere."*

"Please put it on the screen," Matt said as he finished buttoning his shirt.

At first Carey couldn't see exactly what the image was. It was dark. Far too dark to get details.

"What are we looking at?" Carey asked.

"That is an artificial structure," Benny said.

"Can you lighten the image a little, *Star Fall*," Matt asked.

Star Fall did and the image showed a bit more detail.

"What is the size?" Carey asked, "and how can it be seen from this distance?"

"We estimate the size at larger than a normal-sized galaxy," *Star Fall* said. *"We do not know how it could be built or any other details. But it is artificially built."*

Carey just shook her head. There was no way something that size could be built. Of course, she was standing on the command center of a ship that if parked on her home world would stretch from one coast to the other of the United States.

So size in space was only a matter of the time it took to build and gravity and other forces that might tear it apart.

"How can something that massive be powered?" Gina asked.

This time it was *Star Rain* who spoke.

"The shields around each galaxy function to catch energy from the billions of stars in the galaxy and transmit it to the center of the sphere."

On the screen the image of the giant sphere of galaxies once again appeared. And from each one there was a line directly to the center and to the massive structure there.

"Those are power lines," Star Fall said. *"Not dangerous to any ship because of the low level of intensity and the width of the beam that is collected at the center structure."*

"So now we know why all these shields were placed around the galaxies," Matt said. "Giant energy sources."

"Star Fall," Carey said, "How many shielded galaxies are in this sphere and supplying power to that center structure?"

"Three-point-one billion galaxies," *Star Fall* said. "With an average of four-hundred-billion stars per galaxy."

All Carey could do was shake her head.

"We sure we want to get close to this thing?" Matt asked after a few seconds of intense silence.

Benny and Gina appeared back on the screen. They both looked as shocked as Carey was feeling.

"I think we need to go in with more than just our two Starburst ships," Benny said.

Carey nodded to that.

"Agreed," Matt said. "*Star Fall*, what other Starburst ships are close enough to help us out in a five-year timeline of arriving at the massive alien structure?"

"Star Mist *is the only other one,"* Star Fall said.

"Well, that would help some," Gina said. "But looking at that massive thing, I would be happier with all of the Starburst ships."

Carey could only agree with that.

Matt laughed. "Looks like we're getting the old gang back together again."

Benny smiled. "You want to ask them or you want us to?"

"How about we all meet back on Ray and Tacita's ship," Carey said, "and talk about it there? We need to have Ray and Tacita involved with this anyway."

"Thirty minutes?" Benny said.

"I think I can get my hair dry by then," Matt said.

"Star Fall," Carey said, "please inform Chairmen Angie and Gage and Ray and Tacita about the meeting. Make sure you say it is critical."

"Done," Star Fall said a moment later.

"This feel like three hundred years of familiar?" Benny asked, shaking his head.

All Carey could do was nod. But at least they would all be going in there together.

ELEVEN

MATT KNEW THAT Angie and Gage from *Star Mist* would agree. They were shocked, but agreed at once.

And Ray and Tacita were shocked as well, but then promised to keep every scientist working full speed on discovering more about the shields and the entire civilization as the three Starburst ships sent back information.

And before *Star Fall* and *Star Rain* started out, since they were the closest and already on the sphere's edge, they were going to spend a month studying all the galaxies that were inside the shields in their areas.

And study the shields themselves more, to see how the energy was transmitted to the central structure. Doing that would give *Star Mist* time to get to the sphere and start inward at the same time as the other two ships.

It would still take them almost five years to reach the center of the sphere from the edge, all exploring as they went.

Matt just hoped they knew exactly what they were going into by the time those five years were finished.

But he had a hunch they wouldn't. Studying a civilization that far advanced would be like studying magic from a distance.

So finally, Carey and Matt started to settle back into a routine. A new routine, with different worries, but still a routine.

It was over breakfast that Carey said, "You know it's only three days until the start of the Tip-to-Tip. Should we cancel it?"

Matt felt stunned that he had forgotten that.

He munched on a piece of toast for a moment, thinking, then shook his head. "No, we don't cancel it. But we allow this year for teams to substitute if a team member is out on assignment."

"No substitution for injury?" Carey asked.

"No, only assignment," Matt said, smiling. "That way if we are off for a meeting or something, we can have someone run for us."

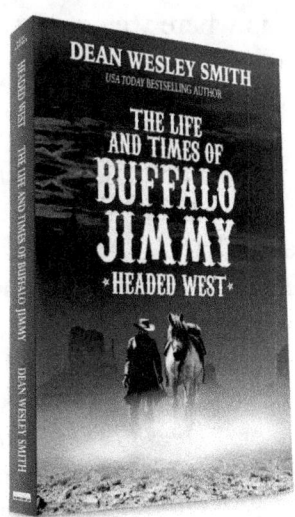
"So if a main team member gets injured," Carey said, "that team has to run nine, but can substitute in those nine for assignments."

"Exactly," Matt said. "Only official assignments, though."

She laughed. "I had a hunch you would say that. I'll get the teams to turn in their ten main runners and ten substitutes by twenty-four hours ahead of the race."

She moved into the other room to contact the crew members responsible for the course and the rules of the race and Matt immediately got in contact with Jacob Stein, the captain of his team and told Jacob the changes in the rules.

Jacob assured him that he could find ten more runners in the two days without an issue. And said he liked the idea a lot.

Matt liked the idea as well. And it would make the ship feel like things were back to normal, even though they were now exploring an alien construction larger than anything he could imagine.

Carey came out of the back smiling. "All set. Glad we aren't cancelling the race."

"Yeah, me too," he said, going back to finishing his breakfast. "Don't know if I can take another year of you gloating."

"Going to have to when we beat you again," Carey said, laughing.

All Matt could do was shake his head at that.

Twenty minutes later they were back in the command center when the reports from other scout ships going through shields and then returning started to pour in.

Matt hated what he was seeing with every report.

The scout ships had been ordered to go through the galaxy shield and remain shielded from anything inside. They were to do a four-hour scan of the galaxy and then report back.

Twenty scout ships had gone into twenty shielded galaxies and came back out without incident. Every one reported that an ancient civilization, very advanced, had lived and filled the galaxy, and then died off.

"What killed this race?" Matt asked as he and Carey sat in their command chair and scoured the reports.

"Maybe nothing did," Carey said. "Maybe they all just moved on to somewhere."

Matt just shook his head at that. Galaxies full of beings just didn't get up and move. Or did they?

"We need a lot more data," Carey said. "How about we send in fifty or sixty scout ships into one galaxy and have them spread out for four or five days and dig up as much information as they can find."

"Agreed," Matt said. "We need to know what killed this race. Or made them leave. Or if the race is completely dead, or just these outer galaxies are dead."

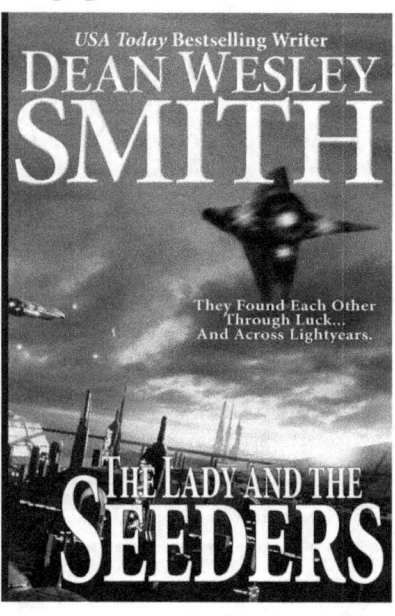

"Or if these were even the same race that built the center structure," Carey said.

"Real good point there," Matt said, nodding.

More and more scout ships returned from different galaxies after their four-hour mission. All were the same, and that worried Matt more and more with each discovery of another dead galaxy.

It wasn't until both he and Carey were about to jump to get some lunch that one scout ship reported in with a very interesting find. They had found an intact space station still in a neutral orbit between two star systems. The station was huge by any standards, ten times the size of *Star Fall*.

Matt stared at the images of the station. It looked alien, yet familiar. It had a massive round center area, with pointed top and bottom that made it look a lot like an old Christmas ornament from his childhood. It seemed to spin slowly on its axis.

"There are still alien ships docked at this station," Carey said.

"*Star Fall,* is the station dead?" Matt asked.

"*From all scans of the scout ship,*" *Star Fall* said, "*yes, it is dead.*"

"There is where we get our answers," Matt said.

"Agreed," Carey said.

"*Star Fall,*" Matt said, "have thirty of the survey ships and a dozen science ships, all with military escorts, descend on that station."

"Have one of their ships duck out of the galaxy shield and report in all progress every hour," Carey said.

"*Assigned,*" *Star Fall* said a few moments later. "*The ships are headed there now and the first to arrive will be entering that galaxy in the next fifteen minutes.*"

"Then we better get some lunch before the show begins," Carey said, standing and stretching.

Matt stood as well. Lunch sounded really good at the moment. But part of him wished he could be exploring that alien station along with the military and scientists. The idea excited him, but that was not his job.

"You know," Carey said, "if we eat quickly we might have time for a short run before the first reports start coming in."

Matt laughed and shook his head. "I think I'll taper down for the big race. Don't want to overdue it."

She laughed and shook her head and damned if he could figure out why.

TWELVE

CAREY FELT EXCITED about the find of the massive alien space station. Anything still in place in that kind of dead area of space still had a chance of being fairly intact, even after such a long time. It would depend on how long the station's shields had held out against the constant space dust.

And what material the aliens had constructed the station with.

But what she really hoped for was an answer, or even a hint, at what had killed all these galaxies full of advanced-culture aliens.

Or even what the aliens had looked like.

She had decided as well to not go on a run after lunch. So after ham sandwiches with chicken soup and tea, they were both back in the command center and in their command chair waiting for the first report and images of the station.

While they were waiting, she suddenly had a thought. "We need to get Chairman Ray to contact the Gray. See if they know about this culture."

Matt nodded. "Really good thinking. *Star Fall*, could you put us in touch with Chairman Ray? Tell him it is not an emergency."

A moment later *Star Fall* said, "He can talk with you now."

"Please put him through here," Carey said.

Chairman Ray's image appeared in front of them, his long gray hair streaming down his back. From the background, he seemed to be standing in the command center of his ship.

"Chairmen," Ray said, nodding.

"Thanks for talking with us," Matt said. "We have a suggestion."

Ray nodded.

"We think it might be a good idea to inform the Gray what we have found and see if they have any knowledge about an ancient race in this area of space."

Ray stared at them for a moment, then nodded. "That is a very good idea. I will do so at once."

"Thank you," Carey said.

Ray nodded and with that Ray cut the connection.

"First report in now," *Star Fall* said.

Carey felt too excited to sit in their chair for this, so she stood and Matt followed her as the first report from the first ships approaching the alien station came in.

Up close images were part of the first report.

"Amazing condition," Matt said softly.

She had to agree, for being there in space for maybe a million years, the alien space station was in fantastic condition.

The first report consisted mostly of a number of scout ships circling the station and detailing it out with scans and images. From what Carey could tell, the scans were able to penetrate into the station some, so they now had some floor plans of the interior just under the shell.

Also, there were five large ships in dock at the station.

"I'm not liking the looks of this at all," Matt said softly to her.

He indicated they should sit back down in their command chair where none of the other crew could hear them.

She did, wondering what he had seen that she hadn't seen.

"Take a look at those alien ships," Matt said. "What do they look like?"

Matt brought up an image of the ships in dock at the station.

It took her a moment, then she realized what she was seeing. They looked like Seeder ships, with the traditional bird-like shape.

"The shape of the station itself is very human-like, not alien," Matt said. "And look at the scans of the interior we are getting in. Human-sized rooms and hallways and so on."

"*Star Fall,*" Carey said, "analyzing the data of the station from the first scans, what is the percentage chance the aliens were human or humanoid?"

"*Taking account of all factors,*" *Star Fall* said, "*ninety-five percent probability the station was human or Seeder built.*"

Carey just sat there in their command chair, her mouth open as more images of the station flashed past.

"*Star Fall,* any idea how long this station has been abandoned?" Matt said. "A range of high probability would be fine at this point."

"*One million to one-point-two million years,*" *Star Fall* said.

Carey just looked at Matt, then she shook her head. "*Star Fall,* any idea how long ago this station was built?"

"*Three-to-five million years ago,*" *Star Fall,* said. "*An approximation. As more data are delivered, I will be able to place that date more exactly.*"

"*Star Fall,*" Matt said, "would you please send all these first scans and information to Chairmen Ray and Tacita and *Star Rain* and *Star Mist.* Their chairmen need to see this as well."

A moment later *Star Fall* reported it had all been sent.

Carey looked at Matt. "What the hell is going on here?"

"Seems to me we might have just found the old home of our ancestors," Matt said. "I wonder if they are still alive and will mind a visit from the family."

"But that station was built more than three million years, long after Ray and Tacita took out the first Seeder mother ship," Carey said.

"Think there is something Ray and Tacita are hiding from us?" Matt asked.

Carey just shook her head. She hadn't been afraid of finding a civilization of aliens. But finding a massive dead civilization of humans or Seeders just scared her to death.

She just hoped they were wrong in their assumption, and that *Star Fall* was wrong as well.

But she knew that wasn't going to be the case.

So now they were faced with digging into the graveyard of what might have been their own ancestors.

She hated that idea more than anything.

THIRTEEN

MATT JUST FELT stunned as he and Carey stood from their chairmen chairs and stared at the large screen in front of them.

It would be another half hour before the next scout ship appeared to give a report. But in the meantime, scout ship after scout ship were going into other shielded galaxies and reporting that formally teeming life was now all gone.

And all of the Earth-like planets that had once been occupied had been terra-formed as Seeders did ahead of seeding a galaxy with humans. But now the planets had swallowed back up almost all signs of any civilization and were lush, green planets, empty of anything but animals and fish.

So far the scout ships had found the exact same thing in almost a hundred galaxies, and not one sign of human life remained in any of them. Something had happened.

"You are being called by Chairmen Ray and Tacita," Star Fall said.

Both Matt and Carey glanced at each other, then returned to their command chair and Matt said, "Put them through here."

Ray, with his long gray hair and Tacita, with her short black hair appeared in front of them. No one else in the command center could hear the conversation or see the other two chairmen.

"How confident of this information are you?" Ray asked.

"Star Fall says it is a ninety-five percent certainty," Carey said, "and we will know more in ten minutes when the second scout ship reports back with new information."

Matt decided to get it out on the line right now. Ray and Tacita had held information before because they hadn't thought it necessary. This might be another time.

"So what do you know about this?" Matt asked.

"We are as stunned as you must be," Ray said and Tacita nodded. "And the Gray have responded and they had no knowledge of any large civilization, especially a human civilization, in this area of space. They said they have never had a ship this far out since they never had the faster drives until we gave it to them."

Matt nodded.

"We are discovering," Carey said, "that the Earth-like planets in all the dead galaxies were, at one point, terra-formed as we do."

Ray looked shocked at that and Tacita just shook her head.

"And the shape of those ships cannot be a coincidence," Matt said. "This civilization was clearly booming when you took the first mother ship to a nearby galaxy."

"If they had advanced trans-tunnel speed," Carey said, "the first Earth would be in easy reach of where we are now."

"Maybe easier," Matt said. "The technology to build this kind of power system to supply power to whatever is at the core of this is far, far beyond our technology now. I can't even begin to imagine how that power would even be transmitted over such a vast distance."

Ray nodded and glanced at Tacita, then said simply, "Find answers. Something killed or stopped this culture or they abandoned it. We need to understand what and why and how."

"Understood," Matt said.

Ray and Tacita cut the connection.

"Seems we scared the old folks as much as we are scared," Carey said.

Matt laughed. "Compared to the people who lived in this culture, Ray and Tacita are kids as well."

"Well, that's got to hurt," Carey said, smiling as they both stood to watch the new data come in from the ancient space station.

And the new data confirmed what they had already really known. Human station, Seeder-like ships. It was going to take more hours before they dared enter the old station, but they would have full scans of it within four hours.

And after that, Matt really, really wanted to know why humans or Seeders would build a massive structure at the center of a sphere that took millions and millions galaxies to power it.

And what was in it.

SECTION THREE
Information

FOURTEEN

CAREY AND MATT had spent the next three hours studying the information coming in from all the scout ships and the information every hour from the scientists and scout ships now surrounding the ancient space station.

One piece of information that Carey felt good about: The station had had no offensive or defensive weapons at all.

And none of the docked ships had either. So this society, at the time of its death, had been peaceful.

Two of the major scientists on the mission felt that the docked ships might give them more information. Starships were designed to withstand long periods of space, more so than a stationary space station.

Matt and Carey both agreed and told two teams to focus on one of the ships and getting into it, and the rest of the scientists and scout teams to focus on the station.

It was very slow going since the military parts of the teams checked everything for any sort of old trap. They found nothing, but they continued to check.

After three hours, Matt and Carey went back to their apartment and Matt cooked them dinner of fresh salads and beef ribs in barbeque sauce.

Reports from *Star Rain* came in while they were eating. The *Star Rain* scout teams on the other side of the massive sphere were also finding galaxy after galaxy of empty planets that had once teemed with human life. So it seemed a logical extrapolation that what had happened to this culture had been throughout the entire massive sphere of galaxies.

All Carey could think about over and over was what had killed them all? Or if not killed, what had happened? Where had they gone?

After dinner she and Matt jumped back to the command center just in time for the next update from the space station.

Ten military and scientists had jumped onto what appeared to be the command center of the largest ship docked at the station.

As they did, the ship had come alive, the lights coming up, some old panels trying to boot up, which had scared them all.

Matt and Carey stared at the images of the command center. It looked like almost any command center on a Seeders ship, with a large chairmen's chair on the lower level, a second level of stations, and a larger third level of stations.

"That design is no coincidence," Matt said.

Carey could only stare and nod. Clearly this race had influenced Ray and Tacita and the early Seeders, more than likely without Ray and Tacita knowing it, just as Seeders influenced human advancement without humans knowing about it.

Carey glanced at Matt. "We need to have Ray and Tacita go back through whatever records of their first flight and the building of their ship and see if they can spot the Seeders from this society in their ranks. Who came up with the ship design for them? And are any of those Seeders still around?"

Matt nodded. "*Star Fall,* did you understand that? If so, please suggest that to Chairmen Ray and Tacita."

"*Sent,*" *Star Fall* said a moment later.

Carey went through the reports as the teams on the ship worked to keep the ancient systems running and see if the core intelligence was still intact.

"*Star Fall,*" Matt said. "If you could contact that ancient ship's systems, do you think you could talk with it?"

"*Unlikely,*" *Star Fall* said. "*But there would be a slim chance of success. I could make the attempt in a clean and secure system, away from all this ship's normal working systems.*"

Matt nodded and glanced at Carey.

Carey nodded. "Let's pull that ship out of the shield."

If *Star Fall* thought there might be a slim chance, and would be safe in the attempt, it might be worth it.

Matt gave the order to pull the ancient ship out of the galaxy shield.

"*Star Fall,* how long should that take to move the ancient ship out of the galaxy shield?" Carey asked.

"Thirty minutes, maybe slightly more," *Star Fall* said.

"This could get very interesting very quickly," Matt said, smiling.

She wasn't always sure she liked his definition of interesting. But in this case, he was right, as if all this wasn't already interesting enough.

FIFTEEN

MATT FELT SLIGHTLY stunned when the ancient ship appeared basically in tow of one of the major military ships. The ship was beautiful, but clearly in the style of the older Seeder mother ships. Only it wasn't as large as a mother ship, more like a long-range scout ship.

It was shaped like a bird in flight as all Seeder ships were, with a rounded nose and black color. Matt wasn't sure if the color was original or part of the aging of a million years.

But either way, it looked impressive and beautiful.

Amazing, just amazing, that after a million years, anything at all worked on that ship, let alone held together. Clearly anything corrosive had been drained away. The scientists who had jumped to the command center had said all atmosphere was long gone. That had helped as well.

The fact that the ship and the station existed at all was a testament to the incredible advanced building and technology of this ancient race.

Two science ships followed the ancient ship out of the galaxy shield and then surrounded it.

Matt knew that they had formed a shield around it to stabilize it and keep any space dust or debris from hitting it.

The military vessel turned and went back through the galaxy shield to take up its station again. Two other military vessels took up positions back from the ancient ship and the two science ships.

Carey and Matt both stood beside their chair, watching the scene on the big screen. There was complete silence in the command center as everyone stopped to stare.

"Star Fall," Matt said, "please stream all of this to *Star Rain* and *Star Mist* and also to Chairmen Ray and Tacita."

"Stream activated," Star Fall said.

At that moment one of Carey's Tip-to-Tip running team members appeared on the screen. Chairman Gregory of the science vessel *Brand*. Gregory was a thin, tall man, with large glasses and a massive mouth that seemed to always be smiling. He was also one of the smartest people Matt had ever met and they were damned lucky to have him and his ship with them on this mission.

Matt smiled at him and Carey said, "Got a fun assignment, huh, Chairman?"

"This is a dream," Gregory said, laughing.

"We're thinking that maybe *Star Fall*," Matt said, "in an isolated environment, might be able to contact the brain of the ship. Opinion on that?"

"Possible," Gregory said, nodding slowly. "We have stabilized the power to the core systems of the old ship and we can provide a link. *Star Fall* might be able to work through that link far faster than any of us could to see if anything is left."

"Any idea as to the language?" Carey asked.

"Early standard," Gregory said.

Then he smiled at what must have been shocked looks on Matt and Carey's faces.

"We are clearly dealing with an ancient, pre-Seeder society here. Ship design, everything. This is going to rewrite some Seeder history, that's for sure."

Matt would have loved to see the looks on Ray and Tacita's faces when they heard that.

"So how long do you need before you want to try this link?" Carey asked.

Gregory glanced at something or someone to his left, then said, "Give us four hours to make sure everything is stable, at least as much as we can do with million-year-old technology."

"When you are ready," Carey said.

"And Chairman," Matt said, "one more question. Any sign at all of what happened to the crew of this ship or the station?"

"Nothing," Gregory said. "Closets are empty and no food remains in storage. Whatever happened did so planned and over a little bit of time at least. And there are no signs of human remains, which in a vacuum, even after that much time, there would have been."

"And the mystery gets deeper," Matt said.

Gregory just nodded.

"Thank you, Chairman," Carey said. "Contact us when you are ready."

She then cut the connection.

The big screen went back to the shot of the ancient Seeder ship between the two research ships. Matt just stared at it. He was having a very, very hard time grasping any of this. He knew Seeders worked at a vast scale, but billions of planets full of people in millions of galaxies didn't just all vanish one day leaving ships and space stations behind.

Where had they all gone?

And why?

Nothing at all made sense, most of all that beautiful ancient ship floating on the large screen.

SIXTEEN

CAREY AND MATT spent the next thirty minutes going over all the data coming from the ancient ship and also the next hourly report coming out of the station.

Then when the information seemed to reach a lull, she reached over and took Matt's hand. "Let's go rest and talk. It might be a long night."

She knew they needed the break, needed to give all this information time to settle in.

Matt nodded and a moment later they were in the kitchen of their apartment. He loved their home, the feeling of safeness it gave them. And privacy.

"Tea?" she asked, moving to the counter to get them some mugs.

"Please," he said as she moved to make herself a cup and he went to sit down at the kitchen table.

"Hard time believing all this," he said after a moment, just staring at the table surface.

She nodded. "And we thought this mission was going to just be routine for a few hundred years or so."

He laughed without looking up. "We got fifty years of routine at least."

She nodded to that.

She tried to let her mind just drift as she fixed the tea and then joined him at the table. He was clearly lost in thought as well, since he was just staring off at the far wall.

She set his tea in front of him and sat in her chair.

"So let me see if I have all this straight," Matt said after a moment.

She nodded. They had solved numbers of problems over the last three hundred years by going through this exact routine.

"We have found a massive network of galaxies that are all shielded. We don't know how the shields work at all, but they seem to be gathering certain levels of power being generated from each galaxy. Right?"

She nodded.

"So they clearly aren't defensive screens of any type since we can move through them without problems."

She again nodded.

"We don't know how they send the power back to the center of the sphere that is the network of galaxies," Matt said. "We don't even know how they manage to keep the entire sphere looking like a sphere with all the galactic shifting that is normal over large spans of time."

"Technology so far past our own," Carey said, "as to be almost impossible to understand."

"We know there is some sort of construction in the very center of the sphere that takes up the area of a large galaxy. We don't know what it is or why it was constructed or even how it could have been constructed. But the energy of millions of galaxies seems to be beamed toward it."

Carey nodded. In such a short time they had already encountered more wonders than she could imagine and she had a hunch the coming mission to the center of the sphere would be full of even more surprises.

"We know that the galaxies out here on the edge of the sphere were once populated by humans and that the populations seemed to have vanished."

She nodded yet again.

"Missing anything?" he asked.

"The why of it all," she said. "We have no reason as to why this was built, and what happened to the populations and why."

"And why they helped the original Earth population," Matt said, "build Seeder ships to move out to other galaxies."

"So in essence," Matt said, "we have a ton of questions and no answers."

"Want to make some guesses?" Carey asked. Sometimes they did that and managed to come across areas that they hadn't thought of.

"I doubt I could make a logical guess at any of this," Matt said. "But I have a hunch as time goes on we're going to find out a lot of these answers."

Carey nodded to that, took one last sip of her tea and then offered her hand to Matt as she stood.

"We have a few hours until Gregory gets back with us," she said. "Let's go take a nap."

"Thinking we might need it later?" Matt asked, standing with her.

"With all this craziness," she said. "You never know. But since the Tip-to-Tip starts in just over two days, I don't want you making excuses about being tired when you start."

"A winner needs no excuses," he said.

"Yeah," she said, pulling him into the bedroom. "Just keep dreaming."

SEVENTEEN

MATT AWOKE TO the page from the command center. Chairman Gregory seemed to think they had the ancient ship stabilized enough for *Star Fall* to try to contact its core.

It had been just over four hours since they had fallen asleep.

Both he and Carey splashed water on their faces and combed their hair, then jumped to the command center. Matt actually, in just a minute after waking up, felt much better. Not at all as overwhelmed as he had felt before. Carey's idea for a long nap had been a good one.

Gregory's serious face appeared on the screen. "Chairmen, I think this might be a long-shot at best."

"*Star Fall* will go carefully and secured," Matt said.

"Anything we get is better than what we have now," Carey said.

Gregory nodded.

"*Star Fall,*" Carey said, "please stream all of this to the other two ships and Chairmen Ray and Tacita."

"*Information going out,*" Star Fall said.

"Please have all your staff and crew off the ancient ship," Matt said to Gregory. "And be prepared to shield against any kind of explosion."

Gregory nodded. "We have taken all precautions. We are ready."

"*Star Fall,*" Carey asked. "Are you ready?"

"*I have created a secure control space in a probe,*" Star Fall said, "*that space is not connected to this ship in any fashion. Permission to launch the probe?*"

"Granted," Carey said.

"*Probe launched,*" Star Fall said. "*I am connecting the link Chairman Gregory has set up to the ancient ship to the computer system in the probe.*"

Matt glanced back at the command crew. "Monitor all systems on *Star Fall* carefully. No slips. Nothing gets through."

The command crew nodded.

"*Link connected,*" Star Fall said.

Silence.

Matt glanced around at all the faces intently focused on their stations. No one seemed to be in damage mode at all.

He glanced at Carey who was staring at the big screen with the image of the ancient ship on it, her expression intent.

Silence.

Matt couldn't remember a time recently that silence had so dominated the big command center. He didn't like it.

Finally *Star Fall* said, "*The ancient ship's name is* Arcadia Case. *It was put into shutdown mode by its chairman one million, one hundred and seven thousand years ago.*"

Matt looked at Carey who looked shocked at that number and the fact that the chairman would put the ship into shutdown mode. For Seeder ships, that was like putting the computer core to sleep.

"Does *Arcadia Case* know where its chairman and crew went?" Carey asked.

"No," Star Fall said. "*But it has told me how Chairman Gregory and his crew can help strengthen the ship* Arcadia Case, *so that would be advised at the moment.*"

"Does it have history of its culture?" Matt asked.

"*It would possibly be able to access that,*" Star Fall said.

Carey nodded. "Cut off your contact and let Chairman Gregory and his people attempt to strengthen the ship per instructions."

"*Connection terminated,*" Star Fall said. "*I have left the probe and told* Arcadia Case *the probe is there if needed for contact.*"

"Thank you," Matt said.

"Looks like we got another bit of information," Carey said. "We now know how long ago exactly the population left."

"*I did manage to retrieve a video link of the chairman of* Arcadia Case," Star Fall said, "*putting his ship into shutdown mode.*"

"Play it, please," Carey said a moment before Matt could.

A surprisingly clear image appeared on the screen of a Seeder chairman, working in the command center, clearly alone.

"Sorry to have to do this, AC," he said out loud. "But this is the best way for you to have a chance to survive."

Matt was stunned.

"Let's just hope the Seeders eventually get here in time to save you," the chairman said. "Sleep well my friend."

At that moment the chairman tapped a screen and the image went dark.

Again silence filled the command center.

Intense, harsh silence.

Matt couldn't believe what he had just heard. The chairman of that ancient ship had hoped Seeders would rescue his ship.

"*Chairman Ray is trying to contact you,*" Star Fall said.

"On the big screen," Carey said, her voice soft.

Ray and Tacita's faces replaced the image of the old ship.

"We know that man," Ray said. "His name was Gulle. He helped in the construction of our ship and was a department head in our science department for over four hundred years. That was almost four plus million years before the time shown on that video."

Matt just stared at Ray and Tacita.

How they could remember someone from millions of years earlier was anyone's guess, but the special Seeder genes they all had to command Seeder mother ships gave them that skill. Matt knew that he now never forgot a name or a face, when before becoming a Seeder, he could barely remember anyone.

"So like we do with human cultures," Carey said, "it seems this culture helped Seeders without anyone knowing it."

Ray nodded.

Tacita just looked shocked.

"So what did he mean by hoping the Seeders got there in time?" Matt asked.

"*Star Fall,*" Ray asked, "would you access the memory of how the Seeders originally left the first galaxy. Show the path of how we were expanding and show the location of this galaxy."

Matt was stunned. The Seeders had been on a direct path toward this area of space when suddenly they turned, eventually ending up in the Milky Way galaxy and now beyond.

"Scout ships would have reached this location in just under eight million years at our old speed," Ray said. "So Gulle must have hoped we would eventually get to speeds we are using now and get here sooner."

"We did," Matt said. "Just not for the reason he thought it would be."

Ray nodded.

"What caused the change in direction?" Carey asked. She just kept staring at the map of galaxies seeded full of humanity.

"Three galaxies ahead had new alien cultures," Ray said. "So we turned to avoid them just under a million years ago."

Matt nodded to that. Ray and Tacita cut the connection and the image of the ancient ship appeared again.

The more information they managed to gather, the more they didn't know.

This entire thing would be enough to drive a person to drink.

SECTION FOUR
The Race Starts

EIGHTEEN

OVER THE LAST two days, more and more information had come in from scout ships finding more and more abandoned and dead galaxies behind shields.

Nothing had been discovered as to the nature of the shields and how they transmitted energy to the center of the sphere. Or for that matter, even what kind of energy they transmitted.

And Chairman Gregory said the repairs to the ancient ship *Arcadia Case* would take four or five more days at least before it would be worth the risk again of *Star Fall* contacting it.

The exploration of the huge space station was also proceeding slowly, without

any large finds at all. In two or three more days they would access the command center of the station and start investigating what systems they could get running again. No one had much hope since the station was in much worse condition than the *Arcadia Case* had been.

So with things once again on a smooth daily routine, both Carey and Matt decided they wanted to run the first ten-kilometer leg of the relay for their teams, just as they did every year.

Carey loved being the starting runner for her team. That was always fun.

The race each year started and ended in the massive lounge in the very nose of *Star Fall*. The lounge could hold a thousand people if needed, and it was the farthest point anyone could get in the front of the ship.

If you thought of *Star Fall* as a large bird in glided flight, the lounge was at the tip of the beak of the bird. That was why the lounge was called The Tip.

Hundreds of comfortable tables and chairs scattered around The Tip and a good hundred couch and chair areas also filled the huge space.

The ceiling was lower in some places and walls of plants in others allowed for much of the room to have a feeling of privacy.

A massive kitchen served the room twenty-four-seven and it was a favorite spot for watching the strangeness of galaxies flashing past in trans-tunnel flight.

Carey and Matt had spent their fair share of time in the big lounge, usually just sitting with a glass of wine staring out ahead as the streaks flashed past the massive ports.

The starting line was flat in the middle of the lounge. A bunch of couches and chairs had been pushed back to form a sort of passageway through part of the lounge and out one door.

One team started every ten minutes to the cheers and support of all of those in the lounge. Each team was timed. Each runner wore a special wristband that allowed *Star Fall* to track the runner's every movement. The wristband could only be taken off and transferred to another team member in a transfer point or in case of injury along the course.

While wearing the band, the runner could not teleport.

Screens all over the ship constantly displayed the location of each runner and their team name.

The course was laid out by red lines along the floors from front to the back of the ship. The course went through large meeting rooms, down narrow hallways, up and down stairs, across major ship hangars, and along major corridors as it wound its way to the very tail of the ship and then came back by a different route, ending in The Tip once again.

Thus the name Tip-to-Tip.

Nine-thousand kilometers long. Each ten-member team had to run nine-hundred ten-kilometer legs. It was a bruising test of endurance, but also a lot of fun. No rules about walking or running. The key was to just finish. Very few teams actually worked to win the race. All just wanted to finish.

Matt's team was called "Chairman M" and Carey's team was called "Chairman C." Only chairmen of ships ran on their teams, so everyone wanted to beat them. That also was part of the fun.

Carey loved the race every year. So did Matt.

They had flipped a coin and Carey had won, so her team got to start off ahead of Matt's team.

"That's the way it will end up as well," she said to him, smiling.

They had both changed into their running clothes in their apartment, then jumped to The Tip. All of their team members were already there and the team ahead of Carey's was just starting off, their lead runner going across the giant lounge and then out through a large door and into a massive hallway, all while everyone cheered.

Carey fitted the official team armband on her arm, then talked for a minute with her team, making sure they all had their times down for jumping to the transition point.

Then she kissed Matt and walked over to the starting area.

There was a timer ticking down and then a loud ding sounded and the light on her armband turned green.

She started off at a fairly good pace as the hundreds and hundreds of people in The Tip cheered.

Then the cheering calmed as she went through the door and out into the

Writing Advice
from Dean Wesley Smith

wide hallway leading from The Tip back toward the rest of the heart of the ship.

The red line on the floor moved at a steady pace under her feet as she forced herself to calm down, slow down, and breathe.

Just breathe.

Damn this was fun.

She wouldn't be thinking that in thirty days if they were still in, but for now she just let herself enjoy the feeling of running through her ship.

NINETEEN

MATT FINISHED HIS ten-kilometer leg just a few minutes behind Carey, even though she had started ten minutes ahead of him. He just had a naturally longer stride than she did.

**Writing Advice
from Dean Wesley Smith**

She knew he was close from the screens in the transition point, so she had waited for him to make the pass-off of the armband to Chairman Aicher.

Matt was smiling just as she was. It felt great after all the stress of the last week to get out and really exercise.

Between nine and ten hours from now they would run their second legs, depending on how fast or slow the rest of their team ran. The first legs were always faster. But then as the team members settled into routines and run-walk legs, the hours between having to run grew, which helped them all recover a little.

At least as long as all of the team members stayed healthy.

They jumped back to their apartment and Carey took a shower while Matt checked to see if anything more had come in from the command center. So far everything was on track.

So far.

Matt took a shower next, then they both sat and had lunch while looking over reports.

There were a couple things that had bothered Matt that he had thought about while running.

The chairman of the *Arcadia Case* had put the ship into shutdown mode knowing he would never come back. That means he planned on teleporting somewhere, assuming the older Seeders could teleport, which it was logical to think they could.

But teleporting to the center structure would be too far, even for Matt and Carey. And if the chairman of the *Arcadia Case* was a normal Seeder, he couldn't jump very far. Not much farther than across the galaxy he was in.

So where did he go? Forget the why, maybe just figuring out where he went and how would give them some clues as to where everyone went. Clearly the shutdown had been clean and planned. Otherwise he wouldn't have hoped that Seeders would find his ship.

A second thought was about the cultures on the planets. Were they all Seeders, or were they all human, or a combination of both? And was it possible, after a million years, to find signs that any part of the cultures stayed behind and survived for a time?

They might get some answers on that after *Star Fall* contacted *Arcadia Case* again. But he wasn't sure if he wanted to wait.

So he told Carey his two thoughts as they finished their ham sandwiches and sports drinks.

"We can send scout ships to take closer readings and looks at a few hundred planets," Carey said. "That might get us some answers on that question."

He nodded. He liked that idea.

"No idea how we go about answering the other question," she said.

"Breadcrumbs," Matt said. "Only think of them on the scale that this ancient society might use."

Carey nodded, but Matt could tell she didn't much like the idea. After a moment she said, "That doesn't feel right. I think there is something we are missing about the shield and the link to the massive structure in the center. We assume it is collecting energy, right."

Matt nodded. "An assumption based on zero facts."

"Exactly," Carey said, nodding. "What happens if those beams are a form of transportation system?"

Matt nodded to that. "Again, anything is possible. As far as we know they might simply be an anchoring system to hold the galaxy in a consistent location with the rest of the sphere."

"I was thinking as I was running how the residents of almost a billion habited planets in just one galaxy alone either decided to leave, were taken away, or died."

"All three of those options scare me in different ways," Matt said.

Carey just nodded to that.

Matt laughed. "And we think we work on large scales."

"Compared to this ancient society," Carey said, "we haven't left the crib yet."

All Matt could do was nod to that, since he felt exactly the same.

TWENTY

OVER THE NEXT four days, Carey and Matt each ran their assigned legs of the race. Matt's team after three days was almost thirty minutes ahead of Carey's team and she kept reminding him that being ahead didn't matter, it was finishing.

Carey was starting to feel the exercise in her legs, but every night she took a whirlpool bath and Matt rubbed her legs down and she did the same for Matt's legs.

They had sent a few-hundred scout ships into three different shielded galaxies to study what bits of the old civilizations were left on the planets to see if they could come to any kind of conclusion.

So far, no luck at all.

It was clear that a large civilization, advanced, had flourished on the planets and nothing much was left of it now. The planets, being healthy, Earth-like planets, had all reclaimed most of what the ancients had built.

There were no structures underground, nothing left at all to show that part of the population had lasted much past the departure date.

And Carey had agreed with Matt's idea to search for some sort of trail leading from any of the galaxies, but as they both had expected, no signs of that at all.

And not one bit of progress on discovering what the shields were, how they were powered, or what the beam was that connected every shielded galaxy to the core.

Finally, after four full days, the ancient ship *Arcadia Case* was deemed stable enough to once again connect to *Star Fall*.

The connection went flawlessly and *Star Fall* reported back that *Arcadia Case* was now systems stable.

Carey felt excited, more than she wanted to admit. She and Matt both stood beside their chairmen's chair, staring at the big board as information from *Arcadia Case* started to flow in. They were also streaming this information to the other Starburst ships and Chairmen Ray and Tacita.

"*Star Fall,*" Matt asked, "Can we break some of this out into areas of questions? First off, does *Arcadia Case* have the history of this culture?"

"*Parts of it, yes,*" *Star Fall* said. "*This culture, in the form of the sphere and Center, which is what the massive structure at the center is called, existed for approximately eighty million years. It took another forty million to build the sphere to this size before that. Those numbers are approximate, of course, since there would be no exact starting date to this culture's expansion.*"

Carey couldn't even wrap her mind around that. She glanced at Matt, but he seemed to be in complete shock, just staring at the information coming over the big board.

This culture, this human or Seeder culture, was ancient. Ancient didn't even begin to describe it.

Finally Carey managed to clear her head a little, then said, "Does it know what the galaxy shields are for?"

"*No,*" *Star Fall* said. "*But with some time I might be able to make extrapolations on some of the ancient technology to help in that regard.*"

Carey nodded. That sounded promising.

"Does it have any idea what happened to its crew, chairman, and everyone else?" Matt asked.

"*No,*" *Star Fall* said.

"Does it know where all the people on the planets went?" Carey asked.

"No," Star Fall said. *That kind of information was not part of its standard operating systems."*

Matt glanced at Carey. Then he asked a simple question. "What is the top speed the *Arcadia Case* was designed to travel?"

"Trans-tunnel thirty," Star Fall said. *"It could go from here to the Center in three hours."*

"Three hours?" Carey whispered.

Matt just sat there stunned.

TWENTY-ONE

MATT, IN ALL his memory, had never felt so shocked before.

After the information from the ancient ship, Matt and Carey had sat down in their command chairs and talked briefly with Chairmen Ray and Tacita.

They both clearly were stunned as well. Matt couldn't even begin to imagine how much, actually, since for millions of years Ray and Tacita had worked to expand the human race, only to discover they were just distant relatives of the actual human race.

They decided that for a full day everyone would look at the data coming in, both from scout ships and from the ancient ship, and then the eight of them would meet to decide what to do next.

Matt and Carey agreed to that idea and then headed back to their apartment to get ready for their legs in the race.

For Matt, the next hour or so of running felt good. Just thinking about moving forward, winding his way through long corridors and then out into the open of the forward military hangar felt good. He was very, very glad that they hadn't cancelled the race even with all the activity going on.

And even though his legs were starting to tire, he didn't much notice and more than likely ran far too fast.

Carey's team had made up a little time on them, so he just waited for her to arrive at the transfer point. As she arrived and handed off her armband, she also looked like she was feeling less shocked than earlier.

It was hard not to be shocked learning that humanity had existed for so many millions of years and that speeds like the ancients used could be attained.

They planned on a five-year mission to the Center of the sphere at half speed. Knowing that a ship could do it in three hours just made Matt shake his head.

And it was no wonder that members of this ancient race could be helping Ray and Tacita get humans going into the stars millions of years before. With that sort of ship speed, this area was not more than a day or so away from the human galaxies. The same trip that had taken *Star Fall* decades to make.

But he had no doubt that the scientists who had advanced the trans-tunnel speed from the old standard to their new speeds now would be here studying the old ship in very short order. And Matt wanted *Star Fall* to have those new speeds as soon as possible. There would be no telling when that kind of speed would be needed. Space was a very empty place. Getting through the emptiness quickly was always a good idea.

He and Carey jumped back to their apartment, took showers, grabbed some quick lunch, then headed back to the bridge. Matt had been right about the scientists working on increasing trans-tunnel speeds arriving to study the old ship.

Two dozen of them were on their way already through the bread-crumb network and would arrive tomorrow.

Carey set up arrangements for them to stay on one of the science ships and to get daily reports on their progress.

At the moment the ancient ship had seven scientific ships surrounding it and a dozen military ships standing off as guards.

Matt and Carey spent the next hour back in the command center going over the data that *Star Fall* had collected from the ancient ship. Much of it was about the day-to-day life of the crew of the ship. And surprisingly, it didn't much differ from what life was like on *Star Fall* and other ships.

Matt wasn't sure what he had expected. It seems that humans were humans, no matter how advanced.

Then *Star Fall* said, *"The Chairmen of* Star Rain *have called for an emergency conference."*

"Now what?" Carey asked, shaking her head as she and Matt moved to their command chairs.

As they sat down and the chairs closed in around them, Benny and Gina's faces appeared. Then Angie and Gage, then Ray and Tacita.

"One of our scout ships has made a discovery we think you all should know about at once," Benny said. "The ship was doing high-level scans of an abandoned planet in a shielded galaxy that was part of the sphere and discovered this."

An image of a desert appeared on the screen in place of the faces. Then the image sort of dissolved, going down into the ground to expose massive caves dug in the sand.

"I'll be go to hell," Matt said.

"That is a Gray city," Gina said. "We had our other scout ships do searches for Gray cities on other abandoned planets and they found them on every one they quickly checked. All were abandoned."

Matt couldn't believe what he was hearing. The Gray lived in this sphere with humans as well, just as they did in the human galaxies. Gray existed under the dry desert regions of human planets. Water was almost deadly to them, even in small amounts.

They were a race that supposedly had helped humans get out of their first galaxy and get stable and explore. But having Gray here as well was a shocker.

"That's not all we found," Benny said. "Once we decided to expand our searches beyond looking for human developments, we also found this."

The desert scene changed to a scene of a vast ocean surface. Most terra-formed Earth-like planets had vast oceans on them.

The image faded down into the water and then to the bottom of the sea and then down below that to show a vast network of very advanced-looking structures,

forming shelters, open areas, and so on, all in water.

"We think a third intelligent and highly-advanced race lived in the oceans as well," Gina said. "These large cities were also found in our quick checks of other abandoned planets. The underwater cities were also abandoned."

At that the images of the other six chairmen returned in front of Matt and Carey. Only Benny and Gina looked normal since they had had time to get used to this information. The other four looked like Matt was feeling.

Stunned.

"We'll get our scout ships on it as well," Carey said, recovering faster than Matt had done. "And *Star Fall*, is there any evidence in *Arcadia Case's* information about the other two races?"

"I will inquire," Star Fall said. *"It will take a moment."*

All eight of them just waited, knowing that a moment for *Star Fall* would be only a few seconds.

"Yes," Star Fall said. "Arcadia Case *shows historical information about the three races existing together for millions and millions of years. Humans, Gray, and the Cirrata."*

"Octopus?" Matt asked.

"Yes," Star Fall said. *"A species of what we call octopus. They advanced into the stars before even the Gray and Humans did. I have no more history on this subject from* Arcadia Case."

The six faces in front of Matt and Carey just sat there, stunned.

Finally Matt said to Ray and Tacita. "Might want to tell the Gray what we are finding."

Ray nodded.

"All our scout ships will search for more information on this," Carey said.

"I will talk with the Gray," Ray said. "Everyone please share data as it comes in on this."

"With the other Starburst ships as well?" Benny asked.

"I can see no logical reason to not share this information with everyone," Tacita said.

Ray nodded.

Matt agreed completely.

The conference ended and he and Carey stood up.

"Star Fall," Matt said, "please play the entire conference we just had for the entire command crew. Then make sure the entire population of this ship knows about the findings."

The image on the screen showed all eight chairmen, then the Gray city, then all eight chairman again, then the Cirrata city.

Behind him the command crew stood and watched silently.

It was hard not to be silent when your entire worldview was just upended.

TWENTY-TWO

CAREY SPENT THE next number of hours, with only a break for food, watching all the data come in from the scout ships, both from *Star Fall* and from *Star Rain*.

Galaxy after galaxy, planet after planet showed the presence of the long-gone three cultures. In fact, it seemed that the ancient cities of the Gray and the Cirrata had stood up better to time than anything the humans had done. But the

Gray cities were under desert and the Cirrata cities were deep in the oceans.

There was no denying that the three ancient cultures existed for millions of years at the same time on the same planets and it is clear that they all vanished around the same time. No idea why.

Not even a theory.

Matt had stayed working beside her until he got a call from his team captain. They had lost a Tip-to-Tip team member to injury and were down to nine, so Matt's running schedule was now off from hers and he had to go earlier than he had planned.

When she jumped back to their apartment to change into her running clothes, he was already done and out of the shower.

"We've switched to a run-walk routine now," he said. "We all have to walk at least half of our ten-k leg each time."

"Did you do that?" she asked as she quickly got into her running shorts and top.

"Actually," Matt said, smiling, "I did. It was my idea, since our goal now is to just finish."

Carey kissed him. "We have moved to run-walk as well now," she said. "Half-and-half as well. Gives us more time to rest between legs with a slower pace and also isn't so hard on each of us."

"You did that last year, didn't you?" he asked, smiling.

She laughed. "From day three onward. Didn't you notice that when your team dropped out we were almost a full day behind you?"

"All I remember is being too tired to care," Matt said, laughing.

"See you when I get finished," she said and jumped to the transfer point.

Carey got there just ahead of her teammate, but she could see on the monitor on the wall that she was close.

This transfer area was right in front of a restaurant and lounge with a wide viewport across the hallway that looked out at the stars. Tables and chairs had been lined up along the wall outside the lounge for customers to sit and drink and watch the stars and cheer on the runners as they came and went.

Carey knew there were still more than four hundred teams behind her, spread out over a vast area of the ship. The customers here could spend days watching the fun.

It was no wonder everyone on this ship loved this yearly event.

The place smelled of barbeque and Carey walked over to a table with plates of barbeque ribs and fries. Two couples Carey didn't recognize sat at the table, clearly enjoying a fun evening.

"They as good as they smell?" Carey asked, pointing to the ribs.

"Even better, Chairman," one woman said. The other three nodded. "Want to try one?" the woman asked.

Carey laughed. "Don't think that would help my running. Besides, no time. Thanks!"

Chairman Annie, Carey's teammate came into sight jogging at that moment from around a corner and into the transfer point and pulled off the armband.

"Watch out for those ribs," Carey said.

"I could smell them for the last half a kilometer," Annie said.

Carey got the band on and then with a wave to all the cheering crew members enjoying their time in the restaurant and bar, she headed out at an easy run. Her legs were sore at first but quickly loosened up and after a short time she enjoyed the run and the walk.

It gave her time to get her thoughts in place. Especially after all the news that had come in today.

One thing nice about this race as well was that she got to see areas of the ship she had never seen before. She and Matt, through *Star Fall,* knew every inch of the ship, but actually seeing areas in person felt different.

And no doubt she and Matt would have to try those ribs. They looked and smelled wonderful.

SECTION FIVE
Headed Inward

TWENTY-THREE

TWENTY DAYS AFTER the discovery of how old the ancient civilization was, and also that three ancient cultures had vanished together, *Star Mist* finally reached the edge of the sphere.

Now three of the Starburst ships were at different spots along the edge of the sphere and ready to move inward toward the Center.

Matt was excited that they now could get started on really finding some answers. He had a hunch that all the answers were in that massive structure in the Center.

He felt better with the three ships going in together. Among them they had enough military, scout ships, and scientific ships to solve anything they ran into. At least that was his hope.

In the twenty days it had been completely confirmed with scout ships over thousands of planets in hundreds of different galaxies that all three cultures had existed on every planet. And from what they could tell, all three cultures had vanished at about the same time.

Also in the twenty days, the scientists studying the ancient ship *Arcadia Case* had gotten more and more excited at the things they were finding. Matt had been happy to hear that the ship's trans-tunnel drive system was basically the same as theirs, just more advanced, and that advancement would be easy to reach given some time.

What had frustrated Matt the most was that they had made almost no progress at all in discovering what the shields around the galaxies were, how they even existed, what kind of energy they transmitted to the Center, or anything.

One scientist had said to Matt and Carey that they were going to have to find a key to the knowledge of shields. The technology was so advanced, it looked like magic to them. Impossible magic.

Matt knew that more than likely all the answers would be found eventually in that massive structure at the center of this sphere. And now they could head that way.

The idea of approaching a massive structure like that scared him and excited him at the same time.

One thing that made Matt happy was that his team was still in the Tip-to-Tip race even with only nine runners. Meetings had pulled him away from two of his legs, but otherwise he had run-walked every leg he was supposed to.

They still had a very long way to go, but all nine of them had the right attitude. But Matt had to admit that after sleeping for a while, he wondered why he was doing this, since it took him twenty minutes to just walk normally after getting out of bed.

Twenty very painful minutes.

Carey's team was also still in the race and his team and her team were actually pretty close in time. Her team had lost one runner on the fifteenth day, so both of their teams were now down to nine.

She also was feeling the pain. He could tell, but she whined less about it than he did.

Both Matt and Carey were standing beside their command chair watching data flow on the big screen when *Star Mist* reported in that their scout ships along the area of the sphere they had approached found the same as *Star Rain* and *Star Fall*.

Galaxies shielded, billions of empty planets inside each galaxy with evidence of a long-ago major civilizations of humans, Gray, and Cirrata.

Now the original plan was to work their way slowly toward the center, taking five years. But Matt had grown to not like that plan. He had mentioned his dislike of the plan to Carey over dinner one night and she agreed.

"Star Fall, please ask the chairmen of *Star Mist* and *Star Rain* for a public conference. At their convenience."

"They are available now," Star Fall said.

"Please put them on the big screen," Carey said.

The faces of her four friends appeared on the big screen. Angie and Gage from *Star Mist* and Benny and Gina from *Star Rain.* All of them were just standing near their command chairs and Matt could see their command crews behind them.

"We're having issues with the five-year plan," Matt said, jumping right into the reason for the call.

He was happy to see the other four nodding.

"Too slow," Gage said. "I doubt we're going to pick up much more information from interior planets than we have already gotten."

"Agreed," Gina said.

"So here is what we were thinking," Matt said. "We send off today a thousand scout ships each with military escorts, headed inward at three quarters speed. They check the path along the way."

All four nodded.

"Then tomorrow," Carey said, "we each send another group of a thousand scout ships and military escorts at full speed to get ahead of the other group and then slow down to scout that area."

"Will that allow us to go in most of the way faster?" Angie asked.

"It will," Matt said. *"Star Fall* calculates that we should all be able to make it to a reasonable distance from the Center in just about one year at just over three-quarters speed."

"Safely," Gage said, nodding.

"Safely," Matt said. "We rotate out the scout and military ships regularly, keep them scouting ahead of us until we get within a certain distance of the Center. Stop at any point if we find something unusual."

"I like it," Benny said.

Everyone nodded.

"So first wave of scout ships head out tomorrow morning at first shift," Matt said. "Second wave twenty four-hours later. Then we follow first shift on the third day."

Again everyone nodded.

"Here we go," Angie said. "Once again into the unknown."

"Seems to be what we do," Carey said.

At that, Matt could only agree.

TWENTY-FOUR

FIVE DAYS AFTER they started into the sphere, Carey hated the call she got from her team captain, Chairman Aimes, while she and Matt were going over reports at breakfast. Her team had lost another runner to injury. They were down to eight with just about seven days of running left. All of them were exhausted.

Carey could remember last year how she felt, but this year seemed worse for some reason. Every time she sat down she wanted to go to sleep. More than likely it was because this year they were also dealing with the amazing discoveries of the sphere and the ancients, as everyone was calling them.

"We going to try to push to the end?" Carey asked Aimes.

"I polled the other six and all of us are willing if you are," Aimes said.

"Let's keep going and we'll check with everyone every day," Carey said.

"Good plan," Aimes said and cut the connection.

Matt shook his head. "First time you have been down to only eight on a team?"

She nodded. "Got any tricks?"

He shook his head. "Not a one. Wish I did."

His team had just lost another runner yesterday, bringing their total down to seven. They were still going as well, but she could tell it was wearing on him.

A nine thousand kilometer endurance race was nothing easy, that was for sure. Every year going into it she was excited and every year at this point she felt like she had lost her mind for even trying this.

Basically she had been running and walking over twelve miles a day, two legs of the race, for twenty-seven days now. And with another runner down, that meant every leg of the race came around that much sooner.

Writing Advice
from Dean Wesley Smith

There were only just over two hundred teams left in the race at this point of the over eight hundred that had started. So they both had done well so far.

"I'm running in twenty minutes," Matt said, taking one more drink of his orange juice and then heading for the bedroom.

"Go slow," she said as he walked away.

He laughed and then said, without turning around. "At this point there is no choice."

She finished her breakfast, put their dishes in the sink and then jumped to the command center. She didn't run again for three hours. An hour before, if she could, she would come back and lie down and give her legs a rest.

On the big screen in the command center was the image of the sphere and the location of the three Starburst ships.

It also showed the scouted galaxies on the path ahead of each ship. So far they had quickly scouted over ten thousand galaxies ahead of the three ships and found nothing at all different.

Nothing. Every galaxy was shielded, every planet that was human habitable had been terra-formed at one point in the distant past and showed signs of three ancient civilizations, now all long gone.

Carey just couldn't believe that some group out of those three civilizations would have stayed behind somewhere. But so far, not one sign of anything.

And the huge Center structure sort of dominated all of their thoughts. With three ships now triangulating scans of the big structure ahead, they were getting a better and better image of it.

And it became more and more amazing and impossible.

From the looks of it from this great distance, it was a giant sphere itself, basically consisting of massive rings.

No one was sure yet, but they felt the rings that made up the center sphere were rotating slightly. Every day there were more guesses from scientists as to what it might be and how it might work, but nothing at all definitive yet. And they might not actually know what the thing was until they got there.

And even at their current speed, that would be about a year.

It was going to be a very long year of waiting. She had no doubt about that.

She didn't notice the passing of time until Matt appeared at her side, freshly showered.

Together they sat down in their command chair and worked over the reports quickly with *Star Fall,* paying close attention to the most forward scouting ships.

Nothing at all had changed since they had started into the sphere. But as the big image showed, all three ships were barely inside after days of travel.

They finished right as Carey needed to go change for her run.

"I'll let you know when I am out of the shower and have some lunch ready," she said.

"As you said to me, go slow."

"Did you?" she asked.

He laughed. "My slowest ten-K leg yet."

She kissed him and jumped to their apartment and then twenty minutes later took the armband once again for a run-walk, this time across a large hangar used for science ships. As far as she could see in the distance, the science ships lined up. Each bird-like ship could hold four thousand crew and families and all sorts of scientific equipment.

Running and walking along the massive ships felt intimidating. Sometimes she wondered how she and Matt managed to stay sane being in charge of such a massive ship and millions of people.

In her ten-kilometer leg, she actually managed to run past sixty science ships. And she still couldn't see the end of the rows of them in sight. And these were just the ones in base at the moment. Thousands of others were on mission ahead of *Star Fall* and would rotate back in and some of these ships would go out.

Seeders never did anything at a small scale. But compared to the ancients, this was a small scale and that just scared her deep down more than she wanted to admit to anyone, including Matt.

TWENTY-FIVE

MATT WAS PLEASED that for the first time in years, both his team and Carey's team were going to finish the Tip-to-Tip.

And both he and Carey were going to run the last legs of the race into the lounge where the rest of their teams would be waiting.

Carey's team had maintained eight runners, but Matt's team had once again gone down to just six, but thankfully the last two had gotten injured on the next-to-last day, so the six remaining could finish it.

Matt's legs felt like rubber bands, but he knew he could make it. And Carey was just a few minutes behind as he entered the large lounge to the cheers of maybe a thousand people.

He stopped running and looked up at the big board showing the racers remaining. Only one hundred and thirty-eight teams still remained. Some had finished already, another hundred were still on the course.

Matt slowed and stopped about fifty paces from the finish.

He had warned his team what he was going to do, so they just kept applauding.

And then, after almost a minute, Carey appeared through the door of the lounge.

She beamed at all the cheering and then gave him a huge smile when she saw him standing there, still on the course.

She actually ran up to him and kissed him to the cheers of everyone around them.

Then he took her hand and the two of them jogged together over the finish line.

He knew his team had still beaten her team since she had started ten minutes ahead of him and this coming year he would remind her of that at appropriate times.

But the idea of finishing together after nine thousand kilometers was just wonderful and the room was cheering and both of their teams were gathering around and laughing and celebrating.

Later in the evening Matt and Carey had planned on taking both teams together out to a wonderful dinner at the rib place they had seen early on. It would be lots of food, some drinking, and far too much fun.

The applauding and cheering had just about died down when suddenly it started up again as yet another runner came through the door and into the huge room, headed for the finish.

And this time Matt and Carey stood beside the finish line to cheer the runner on as well.

TWENTY-SIX

TEN MONTHS LATER, Carey just shook her head when Matt asked her if she and her team were going to run again. He hadn't really kidded her as much as she had expected him to about his team beating her team last year.

And him waiting for her at the finish had been one of the nicest things she could imagine him ever doing.

But now, as the big Center loomed ahead of them, neither of them were certain if they should cancel the Tip-to-Tip or let it happen again this year.

They were still three months away and all three ships were now close enough that weekly dinners had restarted among the six chairmen again, just as they had done for hundreds of years during the fight with the aliens.

Carey had been surprised at how much she had missed those dinners with her friends.

The ten months since all three ships had started toward the center of the vast ancient sphere had gone without incident. Every galaxy, every planet seemed to be exactly the same.

The only difference as they got closer in was that the scientists said the planets seemed to be older and more worn out.

Granted, a million years of just letting the planets grow wild had helped each planet recuperate, but it was becoming clear that the ancient civilization had expanded outward, growing the sphere larger and larger as it went.

One theory going around now among the scientists was that the ancients had simply outgrown their home and moved to a bigger one.

At one point the six chairmen over dinner had tried to speculate how many humans would have had to move in that case. Not counting the Gray and the Cirrata. Just humans.

There were billions of human planets in each galaxy and billions of galaxies inside the sphere. And each planet seemed to have had a full population on it.

The number had gotten so large, all of them had just laughed and given up. One of their ships could have given them the exact number, but Carey knew she didn't really want it.

And she had little doubt that she wouldn't have been able to even grasp it if she knew the number. You start multiplying billions by billions by billions and the number just gets silly.

Yet the scientists think all those people just packed up and moved at basically the same time because there was no signs at all of a war or a plague or anything else that killed anyone.

And the scientists had assured her and Matt that if there had been that kind of problem, they would have found evidence for it.

Along the way they had also found many other intact space stations and hundreds and hundreds of ancient ships.

They got no more information from the stations and the other ships than they had gotten from *Arcadia Case*.

It was now the Center that had them all focused. Being so close now, they could see far, far more detail and the three Starburst ships where compiling as complete an image as they could, adding more and more detail to it every day it seemed.

Now everyone was sure of the structure. The Center was also a giant sphere. But the sphere was made up of six wide rings, all moving clockwise while also turning on their axis slowly clockwise as well.

There was a smaller interior ring and then each ring got slightly larger as it came outward. About a half a light year separated the rings, but with a structure so massive, they looked close.

So the overall image was of a sphere, but it was actually six rings moving all the time both spinning and twisting, one inside the other.

It was the scale of the thing that completely had them baffled. The largest ring could contain the entire Milky Way Galaxy inside it and never touch a star.

The landmass on the inside of the largest ring was estimated to be that of two-hundred-hundred-billion planets. And it clearly had atmosphere and gravity and seemed very earthlike.

A very bright yellow sun-like object of immense size shone from the middle of the sphere, lighting up the inside surfaces of each ring. As the rings spun and the interior rings moved in front of a ring farther out, night dropped over the surface.

The scientists had surprised the chairmen a month ago by saying that the cycles of day and night were pretty standard twenty-four hour cycles on the large outer ring.

But they had no idea what that center object could be or what kept the rings stable and with gravity and atmosphere on the inside of the rings. And no one would even venture a guess as to the material the structure was made from. Forces like what was happening in the Center would tear apart any material the Seeders knew at a molecular level.

They theorized the power somehow being transferred from the billions of galaxy shields to the Center was what kept the entire thing powered, but they had no real idea beyond that speculation.

As with most things they had encountered with the ancients, the ancients had been so far advanced that much of what the three Starburst ships were seeing wasn't really clear to them how it was done.

Not even in theory.

So now, after ten months, with three more months until they reached their positions around the Center, she and Matt had to decide if they were going to run the Tip-to-Tip.

It would end this year just two weeks ahead of the ships reaching their destination.

She looked at Matt and then said what she had been worried about.

"Wrong time for the run," she said. "We need everyone focused on that monster we are facing out there. We can bring the run back when we find stability again."

Matt thought for a second and then agreed. "After all, how often do we get to explore a massive ancient civilization's abandoned home?"

Later that day from the command center, they told the crew that this year the Tip-to-Tip relay race was off. And the reason for it.

Later Carey got calls from three of her teammates thanking her.

And they got no complaints at all. Everyone knew what faced them.

Distractions at the moment weren't what any of them wanted or needed.

SECTION SIX
The Center

TWENTY-SEVEN

THE THREE STARBURST ships took up positions on three sides of the giant Center sphere. Matt had spent most of the last months just staring at it, reading science reports about it, trying to get used to it.

That, he discovered, wasn't going to be possible.

Star Fall was nothing more than a tiny microscopic speck of dust floating near the massive structure. It was impossible to put scale to what he saw.

One of the scientists, a good friend of theirs named Janet, who was from their home galaxy, had tried to give him and Carey some perspective one afternoon.

Janet had said simply, "Imagine the distance from Earth to the sun. That distance would only be one thousandth of the way across any of the bands. So you could start at the edge of the band, travel the distance from your sun to your Earth and still not really have started the trip across the width of the band."

Matt had just shook his head. How could something physical be that large?

Something actually constructed.

Janet went on. "Now, the big ring of the Center would completely encircle the Milky Way Galaxy. And not touch a star on any side. It has a diameter of over one-hundred-and-forty thousand light years."

"How in the world is that held together?" Carey had asked.

Janet had just shrugged and said, "We have no idea. By any standards we know in physical and molecular level forces, that ring, any of those rings, should have pulled themselves apart, let alone ever be built."

"How is it possible that the ring is moving?" Matt had asked, "both spinning and twisting?"

Janet had just shrugged.

So now they faced the massive Center of the ancient civilizations, something so impossible, it didn't seem real. And so large, they had no idea how to even begin.

So that night, all six chairmen got together for dinner in Matt and Carey's apartment. It was Carey's turn to cook and she had created a wonderful pasta dinner with fresh Italian bead, two types of sauce, and a light green salad with Italian dressing.

After they got eating, it was Benny who brought up the problem they now faced.

"How the hell are we going to explore that thing?" Benny asked.

All five of them shook their heads. Matt actually had no idea at all what they should do. Any plan he and Carey had come up with just seemed to be at the wrong scale.

"So what kind of resources do we have exactly?" Angie asked. "How many scout ships, military ships, and scientific ships?"

Matt held up a hand. "Privacy field down." That opened the privacy field around their dinner conversations and their apartment. He then said, *Star Fall,* do you have the exact number of scout ships, military ships, and scientific ships available on all three of the Starburst ships?"

"In all three ships," *Star Fall* said, "there are twenty-four thousand scout ships of various sizes, twenty-one thousand military ships of various sizes, and eighteen thousand scientific ships, again of varying sizes and uses."

"Thank you, *Star Fall*," Carey said. Then she said, "Activate privacy field."

"So we swarm the place," Benny said.

Matt liked that idea, actually. They would first have to test the safety of the entire area, but all of their ships were used to scanning and covering great distances quickly. And right now, what they all needed was more information.

In twenty minutes the six of them had decided on a plan. They would send out probes first, then smaller scout ships, to test the safety of the entire thing. If the Center proved to be safe, then each ship would send out half of their ships at once, with the focus in the beginning on the large ring and anything to do with power generation.

They would have all the heads of the science departments and military departments submit plans of discovery with that idea in mind and the six of them, with the help of their ships would look over the plans.

Matt liked the idea. It felt like finally, after over a year traveling here, they might get some answers.

And at this point, any answers would be better than none.

TWENTY-EIGHT

AFTER TEN DAYS of probes and small scout ships scanning throughout the large, moving rings of the Center, they were ready to launch.

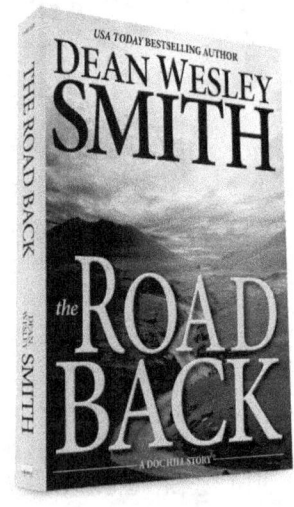

Half of their ships would launch very shortly, spreading out over the largest ring, taking readings.

Star Rain and *Star Mist* would do the same. It would seem like a mist of tiny, tiny, tiny microscopic bugs had suddenly swarmed over the outer ring.

Carey knew that a lot of the crew had issues with the scale of the Center. And many doubted that humans, even ancient humans, could build at such a massive scale, so something else must have built it.

Carey wanted to remind those worried that the major pyramids of Egypt on her home world wouldn't even take up a tiny bit of room on one of *Star Fall's* massive hangar decks. And those pyramids had seemed impossible at the time.

Carey was managing to get a grasp on the size of the Center. Now her interests were moving to how it was built, how it still remained in one piece, and where had the ancient races gone?

She and Matt were in their command chair, hooked into everything happening on *Star Fall.* Surprisingly, all ships were ready, all had their assignments.

And the crews of the other ships that wouldn't go out for a week were all working support functions, from taking in data to helping with final preparations. Not even in all the years fighting the aliens had *Star Fall* seen such a unified activity of its entire crew.

And everyone seemed excited.

All she felt was scared. They were launching just from *Star Fall* over eight-hundred-thousand people into an unknown ancient artifact. So many things could go wrong, she didn't even want to think about it. But her nightmares over the last few days had certainly made sleeping hard.

And every time she had woken up, Matt would be sitting at the kitchen table working over data. She doubted he had slept much at all in the last three days either.

She was sure that many of the scientists and chairmen of ships had had the same problem.

"All ships ready to launch," Star Fall said.

Carey squeezed Matt's hand and nodded.

"Send them to see what they can find," Matt said.

"Launching," Star Fall said. *"Star Rain and Star Mist are also launching."*

For the next hour Carey was convinced that she mostly just held her breath. Military ships led the way on the insistence of the military commanders. A scout ship followed each military ship along with a scientific ship.

Some of the ships stayed higher over the massive landscape of the outside ring. Others dove in closer, moving quickly but recording all the while.

It was those images that stunned Carey in their beauty. Lush green forests, lakes, oceans, deserts, mountains, all there. It seemed that the entire massive ring was covered in an Earth-like atmosphere and settings.

But no signs at all of any humans or Gray or Cirrata.

"There are no ruins," Matt said after a short while. "At least in this area of the ring's inner surface."

Carey snapped her head to look at Matt. Then she said, *"Star Fall,* could you connect us to the other four chairmen?"

The other four appeared on their screen.

"Beautiful, isn't it?" Gina said.

"Stunning and massive," Gage said.

"Seen any ruins or sign that any of the ancients even lived on the surface?"

The other four looked puzzled, then clearly turned away to watch their own command chair feeds.

"No," Benny said. "Unlike all the planets in all the galaxies, there are no ruins."

"No signs of underground Gray cities or under ocean Cirrata cities either," Angie said.

"Well, that's great," Matt said, laughing. "We wanted answers and all we got were more questions."

"Peachy," Benny said.

The other four chairmen vanished and Matt and Carey went back to studying the information flowing in.

The ring itself was not only an impossible distance wide, but it was actually hundreds of thousands of kilometers thick. In fact it was so thick that *Star Fall* could fit inside easily, standing on its tail.

"It's hollow," she said softly to herself, realizing what she had just thought. She looked quickly for at what little data she had about that. Then she said, *"Star Fall,* have numbers of our scout and scientific ships scan inside the ring. What is in there?"

"Understood," Star Fall said.

Beside her Matt nodded, then said, "Good idea."

Less than five minutes later the preliminary scans from inside the massive ring were coming in. It took Carey a moment to understand what she was seeing. Then it became clear.

They had found the cities.

The inside of the ring also was terra-formed to look like the surface of an earth planet, with mountains, lakes, oceans, deserts, and lots and lots of formally human cities.

And unlike the ruins on the planets, these cities still looked maintained.

They were empty of life, but it looked at first glance as if the occupants had left just a few days before.

"So the surface of the ring is a giant wildlife park," Matt said. "They lived inside the ring in another natural environment."

"Looks like there is a sun in the sky down there," Carey said, studying images of one city that seemed to cover a vast area. It had beautiful, sweeping lines in the buildings that seemed to reach into the sky. Stunning, just stunning at first glance.

"They also found Gray cities and Cirrata cities," Matt said, pointing at more data coming in.

Carey looked at the data and agreed. "But where did they all go? And why?"

Matt just shook his head. He had no better answer than she had, which was none at all.

TWENTY-NINE

MATT AND CAREY barely slept for the first two days of the exploration. They did manage to both get regular food and both had taken a nap and a quick shower at one point.

But otherwise, they never left the command center.

Matt just couldn't let himself take a chance of missing something. And with that many ships out, he wanted to be on top of anything that might go wrong.

But the lack of sleep was slowly catching up to him. He could feel it.

The scout ships were starting a giant mapping program to map not only the contours of the surface of the large sphere, but also the cities in the lower section.

The scientists were working on how the entire structure held together and the environmental aspects of holding an atmosphere on the surface of the big ring and also holding an atmosphere and refreshing it in the massive interior.

Impossible tasks everyone agreed. Except for the fact that it was being done right in front of them.

And Matt really wanted to know how the inside imitated day and night, which it clearly did on a regular schedule. Numbers of scientific ships had already started to focus on that.

Because the ring was so wide, the scout ships often reported thousands of human cities as well as Gray cities and Cirrata cities in just one width of the ring. The scouts figured that even with thousands of ships working on the project round the clock, it would take them upwards of two hundred years just to map the insides of the large ring.

And the idea of that excited them all, which Matt found funny.

No one had any ideas yet what was on or inside the other four rings. That exploration was to happen with the second wave of ships going out in five days.

Matt and Carey had had one of the scout ships go in very low over what looked to be a residential area of one city and take photographic images. They had wanted to see what the insides of an ancient's place looked like.

The images were stunning. All the rooms were completely empty and clean. There didn't even look like there was dust on anything. There were numbers of bedrooms with large closets and there was what looked to be a modern form of kitchen. The home had numbers of bathrooms with showers and strange-looking toilets.

"You could just move in there now," Matt said, staring at the images. "Add furniture and a bed and food and dishes and you would be home."

Carey only nodded to that, clearly as bothered by how the place looked as he was.

Matt had no doubt at all after two days that this entire thing was being maintained. They had no idea yet how that was happening. Or even how all the power being beamed at the Center from all the galaxies was being caught and used.

But there was no doubt that massive amounts of energy were being used in just what they had seen so far.

Finally, as things seemed to be dropping into regular scanning for all the ships, Matt decided to ask *Star Fall* one question.

"Star Fall, would it be possible to make a rough guess as to how many humans might have lived on this ring before they left?"

"No," *Star Fall* said, surprising Matt.

Carey glanced at him, also puzzled.

"Can you explain?" Matt asked.

"The interior surface area of this ring would be millions of factors larger than the total surface area of every human planet in the hundreds of millions of galaxies already seeded in human space."

Matt just shook his head at that.

"In other words, far too large for us to grasp?" Carey asked.

"No," Star Fall said. *"Just far too large to try to calculate with any sort of accuracy at this point. An estimate would have no value because it could not be accurate even to the nearest trillion square kilometers."*

"Okay," Matt said. "Thank you."

With that he took Carey's hand and pulled her to her feet.

"My brain hurts," he said. "Let's get something to eat and a full night's sleep."

She only nodded.

With that he jumped them to their apartment.

After some quick soup and crackers, they both fell into bed and Matt doubted that either one of them managed to stay awake longer than a few seconds.

He knew he didn't.

THIRTY

CAREY AND MATT made themselves get back to a moderately regular schedule after the first two days of exploring.

Every night Carey decided that she wanted to cook to get her mind down into details she could handle instead of the massiveness of the Center. That helped her a lot and when she explained why she wanted to cook to Matt, he decided he wanted to make them lunch every day for the same reason.

Staying grounded in their own world was going to be a real task with exploring this massive structure ahead of them.

On the morning of the second week, after all the scout, military, and scientific ships had returned without incident, they launched the second half. This week's task was to do a preliminary scan of the second ring. Smaller than the first ring, but not by much, and the same width.

Carey was almost as nervous at the launching of the second wave of ships as she had been the first. She was starting to completely understand, at a deep level, how really tiny and insignificant they were compared to the knowledge of these ancients.

But thankfully, everything went smoothly and she and Matt could maintain their routine of good sleep and good food, which kept their minds clear on what was happening with the ships.

The second wave knew a lot more about what to look for after a week of following the data from the first wave and what they had found on the outer ring.

From the start, it looked as if the massive second ring was just a replica of the outer ring. The interior surface was like a wild Earth-like planet's surface, with atmosphere and mountains, lakes, oceans, deserts and everything. All completely natural, or as natural as it could be on the inside surface of a vast ring in space.

Inside the ring was where the cities were once again.

And again just one width of the ring would contain thousands of human, Gray, and Cirrata cities. And once again *Star Fall* would give no estimate of how large the insides of the ring were.

The second wave spent most of the week trying to find and study any sort of inner workings of the ring, what kept them moving, what kept gravity on, what kept the atmosphere from just drifting off into space.

They found nothing.

Just structure of some unknown and impossibly strong material and Earth-like environments and millions of pristine, yet abandoned cities.

The third week was when the first wave of ships went back out, but instead of going back to the large ring, they headed for the third ring.

Again, no difference.

And the same the following week with the fourth ring in from the outside.

And the cities in the fourth ring seemed to be no different from the cities in the outer ring.

It was when the ships launched to explore the inner ring that everything changed.

Carey had been afraid of what they would find on the inner ring for a week and all of the chairmen had talked about it.

The inner ring had no forests or land on the surface of the ring at all. It was simply the metal they had found that held all the rings together. This ring had no signs that anyone was meant to live on it.

And the scout, military, and scientific ships couldn't get between that metal surface and the large glowing star in the center.

They could come up under the ring or beside the ring, but not over the ring in any fashion. Strong force fields just stopped the ships cold without any damage.

The inside of the ring was a vast array of massive machines. Most of the machines seemed to be larger than *Star Fall*. After a short time it was clear that billions of beams from the inner ring connected to the large glowing object in the center.

They had no idea what the beams were and they could get no closer to the glowing object in the center.

And no one had the slightest idea even after a week of scans what the machines did. All they knew was that there were more billions of them than anyone could estimate, they were clearly all working, and they were massive in size and scope.

Carey figured they kept the Center going, gathered the energy from the billions of galaxies, but how was so far beyond even their best scientists as to be laughable.

And Carey doubted that the answers of how wouldn't be figured out for centuries, at least. But no doubt this place was going to keep millions of the top

scientists in all of human space very busy for a very long time.

At one point Matt had said, "I feel like a caveman and a plane just flew by."

Carey felt that exact same way.

But there was one other thing that bothered her more than anything about what they had found in the five weeks. They had found no command center.

From how the space stations they had discovered in abandoned galaxies worked, the ancient humans used command centers just as on *Star Fall*.

And all the ancient ships they had found used command centers.

So where was the command center of the Center? She would bet anything it was here somewhere.

But it had not been found, which meant nothing considering the size of everything.

So she offered to cook dinner for the six chairmen. She spent a number of hours on the game hens and sage dressing and

salad. Over dinner they all talked about the Center and all the findings.

But she waited until they were all finished and sipping their coffee before she asked the one question she had been wondering about for days.

"Any idea where we would find their command center?"

That stopped the other five cold and she just smiled at them and sipped her coffee and let the question hang unanswered in the middle of the table.

Finding that command center needed to be their focus and they suddenly all knew it.

And now, maybe they might find it.

SECTION SEVEN
Command Search

THIRTY-ONE

MATT KNEW FROM the instant that Carey asked the question that they all needed to focus their search in some form or another on finding the Center's command.

He had no idea how, but as he thought about it while Carey sipped her coffee and smiled slightly, he came up with a few ideas.

"Any bets," he said, "that the command is in the inner ring?"

Benny nodded. "A logical place."

"But why does it bother me that logic might not be the right answer here," Angie said.

Carey nodded. "I agree. All the rings seem, at least at first study, to be completely symmetrical in nature. A command center would not fit."

"So where is it?" Gage asked. "On that bright sun or whatever it is at the middle of this thing?"

"I doubt that," Angie said, laughing.

Matt looked at Carey as they all sat and thought and drank their coffee after her wonderful dinner. She said symmetrical and she was right. Everything about the entire sphere of galaxies, the Center itself, the interior of the rings, was symmetrical in nature.

"The ancients seemed to take comfort from symmetry," Matt said.

The others nodded.

"Almost anal about it, actually," Benny said. "Gina and I commented on that a lot as we were approaching the Center."

Gina nodded.

"Privacy shield down," Matt said. "*Star Fall*, please float an image of the Center over the table between all of us."

An image of the spinning and twisting rings of the Center appeared. It really was a beautiful thing when looked at like that.

"Please shrink it down to about half the size you have it now," Matt said.

The image got smaller. And if possible more beautiful and stunning.

The bright yellow-sun-like object in the center was now a clear orb, the rings spinning and twisting around the bright center orb like a kid's gyroscope he remembered playing with.

Shrunk down like this it almost seemed possible to handle the size of it. Almost.

"So what wouldn't disturb the symmetry of this beautiful object," Carey asked.

Suddenly Matt realized he knew the answer to that question, remembering how he had taken a string on the kid's gyroscope to get it spinning. The string had wrapped around the pole in the center.

"The poles," he said.

"Of course," Gage said.

Carey nodded.

"*Star Fall,* are there any objects outside the Center above what might be considered the poles of the Center?"

"*Yes,*" *Star Fall* said. *A single artificial moon-sized object holds a stationary orbit over a pole of the Center eighteen light years away from the rings.*"

"Damn," Gage said. "We've been so focused on the spinning rings we didn't look for what was close around it."

"Please show that object as a point of light to show the location," Matt said.

A point of light appeared right above the spinning Center.

Symmetrical.

"*Star Fall,* any other objects like that close to the Center?" Matt asked.

"*No,*" *Star Fall* said.

All six of them leaned forward, then Carey said, "I think we may have just found our command center."

All Matt could do was nod. Maybe now they might actually get some real answers.

THIRTY-TWO

CAREY WATCHED AS the four science ships, four scout ships, and four military ships from *Star Mist* all approached the very large artificial moon above the spinning rings of the Center.

The artificial moon seemed to have an atmosphere and was covered in lush vegetation, some deserts, and a large ocean.

Carey would bet anything those deserts and oceans were for the Gray and Cirrata.

From all scans as they approached, the center seemed to be shielded at the edge of the surface, so nothing inside the artificial moon could be seen.

Carey had a bad feeling about this and Matt had said the same thing earlier. If anything was going to be protected in this massive construction, it would be the control area.

And who knew what kind of protections the ancients had left. But the six of them had agreed that the only way to find out was to send in scout and science ships.

Suddenly a shield appeared between all twelve ships and the artificial moon. The shield glowed orange and gold and shimmered like oil on water.

All ships stopped.

"No damage," the lead military ship reported back to *Star Mist* and Angie and Gage, who were running this investigation since *Star Mist* was the closest Starburst ship to what they all were assuming was the command center.

The lead military ship had come the closest to hitting the shield. Carey was glad that hadn't happened.

"*All three Starburst ships are being hailed by unknown,*" *Star Fall* said. "*The signal seems to be originating from the artificial moon.*"

Carey and Matt quickly stood and faced the large screen. "Please put it through when the other ships are ready as well."

Carey's stomach was twisting more than she could ever remember happening before. They had all talked about the possibility that the ancients would have left behind a message of some sort. And approaching the artificial moon must have triggered it while also triggering the shield.

After a moment a man appeared on the large screen. He was dressed in what looked to be a comfortable pair of cloth pants, a dress shirt, and his hair was gray. To Carey he looked perfectly human and more than likely was.

Behind him she could see dozens of other humans working in a large, but standard command room.

Benny and Gina appeared below him on the right and Angie and Gage appeared below him on the left.

"Welcome, Seeders," the man said, bowing slightly. "My name is Chairman Cannard. We are very happy you have made it. I am contacting you to request an in-person meeting with you six chairmen of the Starburst ships and Chairmen Ray and Tacita. Would that be possible?"

Carey nodded and Matt said, "Yes, we would welcome that."

Cannard could clearly see all of them, so he nodded to Matt's response.

"It would be an honor," Angie said.

"A pleasure," Benny said. "And I am sure Ray and Tacita wouldn't miss it for the world."

The man laughed. "I am sure they would not. We could meet here on the command center. We will drop the screens enough for the eight of you to jump on board. One hour?"

"One hour would be fine," Angie said.

Carey felt her stomach twist down into a knot even tighter.

"I look forward to the discussion," Cannard said.

His image vanished from the screen.

The other four chairmen were still on the screen. "We'll get Ray and Tacita headed this way," Gage said and they vanished.

A moment later Benny and Gina vanished as well.

Carey just stood there staring at the screen that now showed the small group of scout and science ships in space near the shielded artificial moon. She was feeling stunned, completely stunned.

Behind them their command center was totally silent.

They had just spent over a year exploring a completely dead ancient society, and now, suddenly, they found someone at home.

And Cannard, knew who they were and who Ray and Tacita were.

"Looks like we might finally get some answers," Matt said.

Carey could only nod to that.

But she wasn't completely sure she was going to like the answers.

THIRTY-THREE

MATT SUGGESTED THAT he and Carey jump back to their apartment to grab a quick snack. Carey agreed. There was just no telling how long this coming meeting might last.

After the initial shock had worn off, Matt was feeling excited about the meeting. Since they had discovered that the center was completely working and kept clean, it made sense that someone would be here still to do that.

In fact, over the last weeks of their scientists studying the massive structure, one theory had emerged that if the rings ever stopped moving, they would quickly fall apart as well as lose any atmosphere they had almost instantly.

Matt had no idea why the ancients would want to keep the structure maintained and moving, but he had a hunch that they would know the answer to that question shortly.

They split a ham sandwich and a bottle of water, not really talking as they stood in their kitchen and ate. Not much they could talk about. The entire thinking had changed when they found this massive sphere of galaxies and the spinning bands in the center. Matt had a hunch, this next meeting might change it again.

Fifteen minutes ahead of the meeting they jumped back to the command center and checked out all the reports coming in from their ships out studying the center ring.

Nothing unusual at all.

So when Chairman Cannard appeared on the screen and asked if they were ready, Matt and Carey nodded.

"Just jump to my location," he said.

Matt took Carey's hand and they did as the Chairman asked.

They found themselves in a large meeting room with a large oak-looking table and comfortable-looking padded chairs around it. The walls were painted an off-white with large photos of the Center from different angles on the wall, framed nicely.

Nothing at all about the room screamed ancient, powerful, advanced society. It looked perfectly human and normal. Matt actually felt disappointed.

Chairman Cannard stepped forward and shook their hands, saying he was glad to finally meet them. At that moment Angie and Gage appeared and looked around and Cannard stepped to meet them.

Cannard was about Matt's height and seemed totally human.

A moment later Benny and Gina arrived with Ray and Tacita.

Cannard greeted Benny and Gina, saying he was glad to finally meet them, then turned to the shocked Ray and Tacita.

"Great seeing you again, old friends," Cannard said.

Finally, Matt got to be shocked because at that moment Tacita broke into a massive smile and moved forward and hugged Cannard. She actually looked like she might cry.

Ray stepped forward, his smile beaming. "It's been far too long," he said, shaking Cannard's hand, barely refraining from hugging him as well.

Matt glanced at Benny, who just shook his head and shrugged.

"Everyone take a chair," Cannard said, indicating the table. "Any kind of beverage?"

"Water would be wonderful," Carey said and Matt nodded.

As they sat down a pitcher of ice water and two glasses appeared in front of their two seats.

"Now that's nifty," Benny said as water appeared in front of him and Gina as well.

"So," Ray said as he and Tacita sat down next to Cannard. "You've always been an ancient, as we are now calling the races who lived in this sphere."

Cannard laughed, which made Matt relax even more. "I was noticing that new name. I don't feel ancient, but I guess by most measurements I might be."

"So what name do you call yourself?" Benny asked.

Matt loved how Benny could sometimes just get right to the point.

"Humans," Cannard said. "And those of us humans who are lucky enough to have the right genes and can live a long time call ourselves Seeders, just as you do, because of our stated goal of helping humanity spread out over the universe."

Matt nodded to that. He liked that and he could tell that Carey liked it as well.

"First off," Cannard said, "I want to say how honored I am to meet you six. The fantastic work you did to stop the alien infestation saved more lives than I could ever imagine."

Matt and Carey both nodded. Angie said, "Thank you."

Matt was stunned that this ancient Seeder knew about their work.

"Were you and your people and the Gray and the Cirrata watching that fight?" Benny asked.

"Very closely," Cannard said, nodding. "We had no solution to the problem either, but we planned on being there if you could not contain it as you ended up doing."

Cannard turned to Ray and Tacita. "Turns out we sure made a mess of that, didn't we?"

Both Ray and Tacita nodded.

"Our solution seemed like a valid plan at the time," Tacita said.

"It did," Cannard said. "And here at the Sphere we agreed as well."

"So you all started our branch of humanity and Seeders?" Matt asked. "And clearly did as we do on planets, stick around and help us get going. "Why?"

"We are Seeders," Cannard said simply.

Matt sat back, trying to get a grasp of that simple but very complex statement. But beside him Carey seemed to see instantly what he meant.

"You did this not only for our branch of humanity," Carey said, "but for many, many others in the universe. Am I correct?"

Cannard smiled and nodded. "The humans, the Gray, and the Cirrata have spread far wider than you can ever imagine."

"The Cirrata don't seem to be in most of our worlds," Gage said.

"They are there," Cannard said. "You just don't see them."

Silence filled the conference room, so Cannard said simply, "How about I run you through a history of humans, Gray, and Cirrata in the known universe. Then I can answer questions after that on anything you might need to know."

All eight of them nodded.

Matt felt like a kid back in school finally getting to a subject that really really interested him. It was everything he could do to not sit forward in his chair.

THIRTY-FOUR

CAREY JUST FELT stunned and yet relieved at what she had heard so far from Chairman Cannard. And having Ray and Tacita actually be happy to see him reassured her as well.

So now they were going to get a history lesson. A desperately needed history lesson.

Cannard started into the history

"Just under five-hundred-million years ago humanity managed to survive and crawl out of its own solar system and start to explore its own galaxy. As humans tend to do, it stabilized as it filled the galaxy and would have just stayed there if the Cirrata had not visited."

Cannard looked around for a second, then went on.

"The Cirrata, after some initial conflict, managed to convince a group of humans that the universe was a very large place. It was at that point that the special Seeder genes, as we call them, were discovered. When the Seeder genes were activated, it allowed some humans to transport over distances, not age or get sick, and remember just about everything."

Carey had always wondered how the Seeder gene had been discovered. Now she knew.

Cannard went on. "The group of humans in contact with the Cirrata realized that the only types of humans who could really explore the vastness of space were Seeders, so they searched that first galaxy and found about seven million Seeders among the trillions and trillions of human population. And it was on large ships that first groups of Seeders left their own galaxy."

"And discovered the universe was pretty empty," Benny said.

Cannard nodded. "Very empty. So it was during this first half million years of exploration that the Seeders figured out that their main driving force would be to seed humans in all the empty galaxies. It took almost a million years more of trying and failing many times to get to the system you still use now with terra-forming and then seeding and then staying with each culture to help them over the roadblocks."

Ray and Tacita just shook their heads, clearly more stunned than Carey was feeling.

"So why did you let us just go on without telling us the origins?" Tacita asked.

Cannard held up his hand and smiled. "Still got a little more of the story before I get to that."

Tacita nodded and sat back.

"For millions more years the Seeders spread humanity through galaxy after galaxy. At one point along in there they met the Gray, who were out exploring galaxies and also putting their people on new planets. At that point the Seeders, the Gray, and the Cirrata all agreed to work together and keep the Gray cultures and the Cirrata cultures secret from the human cultures developing on the land."

Carey noticed that all of them were nodding.

Cannard went on. "This seeding continued for another ten million years before

it became clear that Seeders needed a home area of their own. So many humans with the Seeder genes were just not being found on the billions of developing worlds."

"So you built this sphere?" Benny said.

"The construction of the Center, which was to be the home world, only took over two million years and pushed our skills to new levels," Cannard said. "We realized it was good for us, just as the war with the aliens advanced your technology."

Carey nodded to that as well. Just discovering the plague of a runaway human experiment sent Seeders scattering to invent entire new levels of technology to help in the war. And it also pushed them to find Seeders on planets where before they would have just been left to live a human life.

So she completely understood a major construction challenge doing that as well, especially something as large as this Center.

"We shielded all the galaxies for power," Cannard said, "and Seeders from all over human-occupied space came here to live in the wonderful society of the rings."

"But you kept expanding," Matt said.

Carey had been thinking the same thought.

"More millions of years went by, more areas of the universe were being seeded, thus millions more Seeders were found and came here to learn and live. At one point in time we had seven hundred galaxies being seeded at any given time."

"Are the Starburst ships going to run into those already seeded human areas anytime soon?" Ray asked.

"Not in your planned five hundred year missions at the speeds you are traveling," Cannard said. "That covers not even a measurable fraction of the universe we know about. And the universe just continues on far beyond what we can see."

Carey just shook her head at that. Sometimes simply understanding space and the vastness of space was just too much to try to grasp.

"So everyone who lived here were Seeders?" Gina asked.

"Yes," Cannard said. "Any Seeder couple who got pregnant moved to a human planet to have the child just in case the child didn't have the Seeder genes. Most children were Seeders and the family returned after the child was born."

Carey understood that. *Star Fall* had many, many families on it, but all the children were Seeders as well.

"So what happened?" Gage asked. "Where did you all go?"

"Getting ahead of my story again," Cannard said, smiling. "After the rings started to slowly fill up, which took millions and millions of years, the desire to seed new galaxies fell off. Living here was just very, very pleasant and fewer and fewer wanted to leave. Eventually groups started to settle on planets in the shielded galaxies and those over millions of years also started to fill up.

"The largest traffic we had in and out of here wasn't the ships leaving on seeding missions, but the massive ships bringing millions and millions of new Seeders here. You all know that every generation on every human planet creates more humans with the Seeder genes. We believed that every Seeder should be found."

"So the desire to create new galaxies full of billions of human worlds faded," Matt said, "as the population continued to grow here?"

"Yes," Cannard answered. "So about ten million years ago we realized we needed a much bigger and better home. So we started the planning."

"And this is where we come in, isn't it?" Ray said.

Cannard nodded. "While the new home was being designed and built, challenging us yet again, all seeding had basically stopped. Many of us thought that against the very nature of who we were. And the Gray and Cirrata were not pleased as well. They needed places to put their growing populations and our terra-formed planets were perfect locations for their populations."

"So you started one planet in one galaxy," Ray said, "and nurtured us to take up the task."

Cannard smiled. "Actually, we started six hundred single planets and did the same thing. All scattered vast distances apart in our known space. There are six hundred different Seeder groups that know nothing of this Seeder home world area."

"We were simply the closest," Matt said.

Cannard nodded. "We hoped you would find this and we helped you where we could."

"Why would you want us to find this?" Matt asked.

Cannard smiled. "Seemed like waste of a perfectly good home to not have someone living in it."

All Carey could do was stare at him.

THIRTY-FIVE

MATT JUST FELT stunned at how much longer the Seeders had been around than any of them thought. He had sort of assumed that Seeders like Ray and Tacita were rare because of how old they were, but clearly they were not.

Cannard clearly had been around long before Ray and Tacita were born.

And the fact that this place had been saved to be a home for a second generation of Seeders stunned Matt as well.

"So how about we get some dinner and then I'll give you all a tour of this base and the command center," Cannard said.

"Can we tell our ships we are fine?" Gage asked.

"Be my guest," Cannard said. "Third shield down."

Carey told *Star Fall* they were fine and the meeting was going to continue. Benny did the same for *Star Rain* and Gage did the same for *Star Mist*.

When they finished, Cannard said, "Third shield up."

"If you know us so well and know that we are Seeders," Benny asked, "why the shields?"

Cannard laughed. "It has nothing at all to do with you. This center is triple shielded at all times. Always has been. We only made the exterior shield visible to you before your scout ships hit it is all. And it is the shield that also blocks transmissions."

"Why?" Angie asked.

"Because without this command," Cannard said, "Those rings out there would stop turning and quickly disintegrate. And the power from all the galaxies would lose focus and the shields around the galaxies would fail. If that would have happened with the rings occupied, the loss of life would have been untold. This small moon, which we call Command, is never not shielded in all forms. And never not occupied by about three million Seeders."

"Even now after all the others have left?" Gina asked.

Matt just glanced at Carey and then back at Cannard.

"Even now," Cannard said. "We have staffed Command for all that time hoping that some day you would find this wonderful home."

"And the only reason you left is because you simply outgrew it?" Matt asked.

Cannard nodded. "The only reason."

"I can't even imagine the size of your new place," Benny said, shaking his head.

Matt couldn't either.

"It makes this place look tiny," Cannard said, laughing.

With that he ordered that food be delivered and it appeared on the table in front of them, including place settings and numbers of different choices of courses and drinks.

The fantastic smell of fresh bread, fried chicken, and prime rib just overwhelmed Matt and he realized how hungry he was.

"Wow," Benny said, "You can serve a meal."

"I want to know how the food just appears," Angie said.

"Yeah, interested in that was well and not just for food," Carey said.

Matt had been wondering the same thing.

"One of those inventions we can help you get to over time," Cannard said. "We had to invent it to build this place."

So Cannard dug into the food and that got the rest of them moving as well, passing around plates like it was a big party.

Finally, as everyone was eating, Angie asked a simple question, or at least Matt thought it was a simple question.

"How do the three of you know each other?" Angie asked.

Ray smiled at Cannard. "He was our second-in-command for almost nine hundred years."

Cannard smiled. "Those were wonderful times."

"Even with the slow speeds and the secrets you were keeping?" Benny asked.

"I didn't mind the slow speeds because I was with wonderful people," Cannard said.

Matt looked at Ray and Tacita and they both looked sad. Cannard looked down at his plate and focused on the food.

"Too much to ask what happened?" Gina asked. "If too personal, please just say personal and we will move on."

"I lost Este, my wife," Cannard said.

"A freak accident," Ray said.

Matt thought Tacita might actually cry, even after what had been millions of years. Clearly the Seeder memory made bad memories as clear as good ones.

"I had to take a break so I came back here and started to work with Command," Cannard said. "But I kept a close eye on your progress and eventually became in charge of the Seeders helping your group."

"But you stayed out of sight?" Ray said. "We missed you."

"I know," Cannard said, staring at what food was left on his plate for a moment.

"Can I ask if you moved on?" Tacita asked.

Cannard nodded. "About two million years ago I met a wonderful partner named Marie."

Ray frowned. "Why isn't she with us now?"

"Yes, please," Tacita said.

Cannard beamed. "I would love to have you all meet her." He looked up just slightly. "Marie, we would love to have you join us."

At that moment a beautiful woman appeared beside Cannard and he stood.

Marie had long silver hair and large brown eyes. She stood not much over five foot and wore a dress blouse with light blue jacket over it and jeans.

"My wife and partner," Cannard said, "Marie Koddest."

Cannard introduced the six chairmen of the Starburst ships first, then said, "And this is Ray and Tacita."

Both Ray and Tacita stood and moved to greet her.

Tacita hugged her, which surprised Matt for the second time in just a few hours.

Marie was beaming. "I have heard so many wonderful things about you both."

"And we are looking forward to getting to know you," Ray said, smiling.

With that a chair appeared beside Cannard and another plate and settings appeared on the table and everyone sat back down and went back to eating.

Matt just stared at the two couples as they laughed and talked. Then he glanced at Carey and then at their four closest friends. They had only been all together for just over three hundred years.

He was just starting to understand how special having hundreds of years to form friendships really was.

SECTION EIGHT
Decisions

THIRTY-SIX

CAREY WALKED HAND-IN-HAND with Matt as they took the tour of the large moon that served as command for the Center. It was far larger than their own Starburst ships and along the way they got to meet many of the crew.

They saw vast hangars full of clearly Seeder ships in the older styles, both research and scout, and vast green areas and also small cities that seemed to exist in forms of domes inside the moon, giving the people who lived there a sense of community and surface living.

On Starburst ships they made no attempt at any of that and Carey found the thinking interesting at best and fascinating at the same time. There was no doubt that if they got a chance, it was an area of thinking of the ancients that she planned on looking into.

And she also found it interesting that there were no Gray or Cirrata control areas for the Center. From what Cannard said, they had seeded the working control of the Center rings to humans.

The tour ended with them in the actual command center.

It was massive, the same layout as the command center in their ship. A dual chairman's chair was the only thing on the lower level, but from there were five levels behind the chairman's level with over a hundred stations, all occupied.

"At one point," Cannard said, "this center held the responsibility for the lives of vast populations of humans, Gray, and Cirrata."

"A frightening responsibility," Ray said.

Cannard nodded. "It was."

Carey only had a faint idea as that scope. She and Matt were responsible for three million humans. That kept her awake many nights as it was. She couldn't imagine working in this room with the rings fully occupied. It would take a certain type of person, of that there was no doubt.

And the fact of so few taking care of so many really bothered her at the same time.

What she found even more amazing is that even with the vast scale of the Center, a structure larger than even the Milky Way Galaxy, it all boiled down to one large room and about a hundred people to run it.

Seeders may do things on vast scales, but it always came back to the humans involved.

After the tour, Cannard promised more information would be coming in the following days. The six chairmen went back to their ships and Ray and Tacita stayed in the Center Command with Cannard to have dinner and catch up on millions of years missed.

Carey just couldn't imagine that conversation.

Along the way Ray and Tacita had seen other old friends and it seemed that they knew half of the command crew. Clearly the ancients had stayed with Ray and Tacita and really helped in the early expansion of the Seeders.

So now the question was would the ancients stay with them now and help them learn all this advanced technology?

Carey sure hoped so.

She and Matt made sure all the reports were looking fine, then told their command crew a short excerpt of the meeting and said they would explain more as soon as they knew more.

"Basically," Matt said, "There are millions of Seeders on that artificial moon and they are there to keep this thing going."

With that, she and Matt went back to their apartment. Matt thought that the only logical thing to do was to watch a movie and just let their minds process what they had heard and discovered.

Carey loved that idea and about halfway through the movie she dozed off.

Matt woke her to come to bed and the next thing she remembered it was time to get up. She really had been that tired.

THIRTY-SEVEN

MATT WAS GLAD that he and Carey had basically tried to focus on something else for the evening. His mind had been overloaded and he knew decisions would not be good ones in that state.

But now, as he cooked them both breakfast, they talked about everything from yesterday and he felt like he was thinking again.

"Two areas that are bothering me," Matt said as he put scrambled eggs and toast and orange juice in front of Carey.

Carey laughed. "Only two?"

"Well, two things past the assumption that we are going to eventually learn all this unknown and magical stuff here and the ancients will stay around and help us."

She nodded to that and dug into the eggs as he went back to dish up his breakfast. He could make the best and lightest scrambled eggs she had ever tasted and loved it when he made them.

"The first thing that bothers me is that they believed that all humans with the Seeder gene should be basically taken out of the human populations and brought here. That's what eventually caused the overpopulation. Right?"

"I think that is right," Carey said.

"So do you think we should be doing that with the millions of galaxies full of worlds we have already seeded?"

She looked up at him and shrugged. "I honestly don't know. Maybe some way to give every person with the Seeder gene a choice might be appropriate. Tough question because who is to say our way is better than not being a Seeder."

"Exactly," Matt said, taking his plate and going to the table.

"So what is the other thing that bothers you?" she asked.

"The other six hundred groups of Seeders and human worlds," Matt said. "Do we search them out or do we just let them go on without ever knowing about this place and their own history?"

"You know," Carey said, looking up at him and smiling, "in a situation with almost impossible questions and challenges, how is it that you can come up with two even more impossible questions?"

Matt just shrugged and laughed. "Thought you liked that about me."

She smiled. "Didn't say I didn't like it. Just wondering how you do it."

"Honestly," he said, "I don't know."

Thirty minutes later they were back in command and going over all the reports from the last hours. No word at all from Ray or Tacita or Cannard.

After they looked at all the reports on the center ring, Matt glanced at Carey. "I think we should just pull in all our ships. At this point they aren't getting much or understanding anything about that center ring. I think we're going to learn a lot more working with the Seeders on the Command moon."

Carey nodded. "I agree.

A couple minutes later Benny and Gina and Angie and Gage all agreed and the order to pull back all ships was given.

Four hours later Matt felt much better that all their ships were safely back on board. And still no word from Ray and Tacita.

So he and Carey went to get some lunch and then were back in the command center an hour later when Ray and Tacita and Cannard finally asked for a meeting with the six of them.

This time the meeting was to be in the meeting room of *Star Rain*.

He and Carey jumped to the meeting room on *Star Rain* just as the others arrived as well.

Ray and Tacita actually looked happy and Marie was with Cannard and they both looked happy.

As all ten chairmen took their seats, Ray said, "For Tacita and me this has been a wonderful reunion with old friends. But I imagine for you six, the questions about what next are swirling."

"That and a few thousand more," Benny said.

Matt laughed. He felt exactly the same way.

"So we have decided to leave those decisions up to the six of you," Ray said. "From this point going forward."

Matt sat back and Carey reached over and touched his hand.

"The six of you basically saved all of humanity from a disaster with your work in the alien plague," Ray said. "Compared to us, you are all very young and still have the sense of youth and the future about you."

"Very much so," Cannard said. "We have been impressed as to how you six brought your ships forward exploring the sphere, yet did it without any major risks to your people."

"So," Ray said, "as Tacita and I did in the war, we will step back and just do as you ask."

"And the entire crew of the Command of the Sphere will be at your disposal," Cannard said. "We will teach you and train you and your people in everything we can, but realize such training may take centuries in many areas."

"And what happens if we don't do something the way you think it should be done?" Benny asked.

Matt nodded, as did Carey.

"We will explain our position," Cannard said. "But the final decisions will be up to you."

"But there is only one area we cannot help you with at the moment," Marie said. "We cannot give you the location of our new home just yet. In time, yes, but not now or for maybe millions of years into the future."

"And the reason for that is what?" Angie asked a second before Matt could.

"We hope that your generation of Seeders and humanity and Gray and Cirrata," Cannard said, "will remain independent from our generation, the Ancients as you call us. Besides the interaction here with the Command crew and scientists."

"We are no longer Seeders," Marie said. "We hope you never reach that point in your society where you become so complacent that you no longer want to explore and expand and help start new cultures."

"And you don't want to contaminate us is what you are saying," Matt said.

Cannard and Marie both nodded. "But we will teach you anything we know that you would like to learn."

"Got to admit that food thing is pretty cool," Gina said.

With that, they all laughed, even though the weight of seemingly the universe had just been dropped on their shoulders.

THIRTY-EIGHT

CAREY SAT AT Angie and Gage's kitchen table in their apartment on *Star Mist.* Angie was cooking the six of them all dinner, from the smells of it a wonderful chicken dish with what looked to be a white sauce. All of them could cook, but Angie was the best.

Angie and Gage's apartment was laid out as Carey and Matt's apartment, but with very different tastes in furniture. They had a darker leather furniture and dark cherry wood for the table and end tables. And had rustic log beams on the ceiling and log posts at different places around the apartment, giving the feeling of a mountain lodge, which sort of fit the place they met as Carey understood.

Angie and Gage were not as neat as Carey and Matt were. They had books and reading pads and blankets scattered around the living room, showing that they spent a lot of time in front of their massive stone fireplace.

Matt sat beside Carey. Benny and Gina were across from Gage and where Angie would sit when she finished cooking.

"So now what the hell are we going to do?" Benny asked after they all got their drinks.

Carey, after Matt's questions earlier, had a few ideas, so since no one else was saying anything after Benny's question, she said simply, "I might have a few starting points."

"Oh, thank heavens," Gina said and they all laughed.

At that moment Angie brought a large basket of butter-covered breadsticks to the table. The smell was to die for, making Carey realize how hungry she actually was.

"Dig into those," Angie said. "I have more with dinner which is still about fifteen minutes."

Angie took one and turned to go back to the counter while the rest of them took a warm breadstick.

The thing melted in Carey's mouth it was so good.

Benny actually sighed after taking a bite of his.

"So first off," Carey said, "I'm thinking all our ships have to be upgraded for speed."

"And for the new shields needed to handle that speed," Matt said.

They all nodded.

"So just as we did with the alien fight," Carey said, "how about we take over a few planets here in the sphere and set up factories to upgrade all of our ships."

"I like that," Benny said. "And Gina, I flat love these bread things."

"Thanks," Angie said from the kitchen area. "And I love Carey's idea as well. That will give us a focus and after we are finished a far greater freedom of movement."

"I would say that after we learn the new speed upgrades, we also pull back all the other Starburst ships to the Milky Way," Gage said, "and convert the major shipbuilding facilities there to deal with the new speed and shields as well. Upgrade every Seeder's ship over the next one hundred years."

"That's a lot of ships," Benny said. "But if we think like the Ancients and think big, I bet we can do it."

"So do I," Matt said, nodding.

Carey liked that a lot. Clearly they were all in agreement. But she had one more thing she had to say and she wasn't sure what her friends were going to think about this.

"I have another thought," Carey said. "I have never stood on the surface or inside one of those rings, so I don't know how I would honestly feel. But it scares hell out of me that only a hundred or so people can hold that many lives in their hands."

"Oh, thank heavens I wasn't the only one that felt that way," Gina said.

"Make it three," Angie said from the kitchen.

All three men raised their hands, smiling in agreement.

Carey nodded. That made her second suggestion a more likely solution.

"So before we let anyone get near those rings," Angie said, "we fix that problem. Damned if I know how. That would be up to the scientists, but we need to fix it."

"And we fix the fact that those screens around galaxies can't be really seen through enough," Gage said. "We have to make them invisible."

Everyone nodded to that as well.

"You know," Benny said, "I used to hate moving into someone else's old house."

Carey felt the same way and that was her second suggestion. Matt was nodding.

"The Ancients have flat said that living in those rings caused them to grow stagnant," Carey said. "So even if we could fix the safety issue, not sure we would want to move Seeders into the rings."

"You thinking we just shut it down?" Angie asked, bringing in a bowl of fresh salad and putting it in the middle of the table.

"Not so much shut it down," Carey said. "Fix the safety issues, sure, and the screen issues, but then maybe find another purpose for it."

Matt laughed. "Seems like the purpose would be obvious."

Everyone sort of looked at him. Carey could see the glint in his eye, which meant he had the most obvious solution to something that should have been obvious to all of them.

"We seed it," Matt said, smiling. "Let humans and Gray and Cirrata have it."

"Duh," Benny said, shaking his head.

Carey laughed and everyone applauded.

Matt took a pretend bow. And at that point Angie got Gage to help her serve dinner.

Carry had no doubt Matt's idea was a perfect one for the Center and all the galaxies around the Center. But there were so many more things to deal with.

And that would take time, something Seeders clearly had in abundance.

THIRTY-NINE

OVER THE NEXT six months, Matt felt as if they were back in the early days of the alien war effort. Scientists were poring through the breadcrumb network from human space to learn from the Ancients.

And the scientists who had been here for over a year studying the drives on *Arcadia Case* had already made headway and now with the Ancient engineers in Command, they believed they would be ready in just six months to retro-fit the first Seeder ship and test it.

From the reports Matt saw and from what *Star Fall* explained to him and Carey, once the retro-fits started, it would go quickly. In fact, *Star Fall* felt that its engines could be done safely and tested in under a month.

The six of them had not mentioned their plan for the Center to anyone else. They wanted to hold on that until they had most of the more advanced technology.

And all of them had agreed that the military ships would remain a part of Seeder culture going forward. Matt was very happy they had all agreed on that because having the military there made everyone feel safer. The universe seemed to be a never-ending place, from what the Ancients hinted at, so better to be safe than sorry later considering how far out they planned to go over the centuries coming up.

The six of them had decided to have dinner together two nights a week now. And they had some great discussions, not the least of which was about what to do with Seeders left on human planets to live as humans.

Not a one of them had an idea about any long-term plan, but all of them sort of agreed that each Seeder should be made aware of their genes and given the choice. And that would entail a massive new Seeder department that they would set up sometime in the very near future.

Matt could only imagine being a member of that department, having to talk with people who thought they were just normal people, living their lives, and then suddenly learn they had special genes that would allow them to live forever, never be sick, have a stunning memory, and travel long distances in space if they wanted the genes activated.

Gage had said that department would be exploring really, really strange new worlds. Matt agreed completely there.

They all six agreed that Seeder mother-ship production should be increased. They told Cannard that decision and he and Marie just beamed. It seemed that it really bothered the Ancients that they had lost the desire to seed humanity through the stars.

The biggest discussion the six of them had was about the other major groups of Seeders out there. Six hundred groups in theory. But who knew how many splinter groups off the original six hundred.

And if each group of Seeders had moved the way Ray and Tacita's group had moved, there were more billions of human galaxies out there than anyone could imagine.

The six of them were pretty much in agreement that they should find and contact the other groups. But how and when was where all agreement broke down.

Thankfully, it wasn't something that needed to be decided at once.

But for some reason Matt kept coming back to that issue. It ate at him, as if something was very wrong but he couldn't put his finger on it. So one evening he suggested to the other chairmen that they have a meeting with Cannard and Marie and ask them if they have kept track of the other six hundred groups as they did with Ray and Tacita's group.

All six agreed, so the next day they requested a meeting with Cannard.

They ended up back in the meeting room on *Star Mist*.

After Cannard gave them an update about how excited his engineers and scientists were working with the Seeder engineers, he smiled and said, "I have a hunch this meeting has a direct point."

"It does," Matt said, taking the lead since this bothered him the most. "We are wondering if you and your people kept as good of track on the other six hundred Seeders groups you started as you did ours."

Cannard shook his head. "We did not, I'm afraid. Many of them are extreme distances away, even with our speeds. We basically seeded one planet and left ships to help them get into space and learn how to activate their Seeder genes. And we guided each culture to becoming Seeders.

But after they had seeded the first few galaxies and were moving forward, our ships returned home."

Matt sat back. That was the worst answer Cannard could have given.

Beside him Carey had gone white and Benny was just shaking his head.

None of the six of them said a word.

After a moment Cannard said, "I see my answer upset you all. Can I ask why?"

"We just spent three hundred years fighting a human experiment gone bad," Matt said.

"If we had not contained that alien experiment," Benny said, "It would have eventually reached here long after taking out all of human space."

Cannard sat back, clearly realizing what they were saying. Matt found it interesting how Ancients could sometimes not see obvious things right in front of them. Ray and Tacita had had that problem a few times as well.

"We need to find those other Seeder groups and do it fairly quickly on the scheme of things," Benny said.

"Very quickly," Matt said. "We don't need to tell them we are here or even introduce ourselves, but we need to know what is happening with each group. See if they are still alive or have started something like we started with that alien experiment."

Cannard nodded. "I will get you the locations of their origin galaxies seven million years ago. I am sure your ships can update for galactic shift over time and locate them. But again, distances are extreme."

Carey looked at Matt and smiled. "So we make our ships even faster."

"Well, that will be a challenge for not only our engineers, but yours," Benny said to Cannard.

All Cannard could do was sit there looking a little stunned.

That was the problem with putting kids in charge of the store. Innovation was difficult to those stuck in the old ways.

Especially ways that were millions of years old.

FORTY

OVER THE NEXT two months the pace of everything picked up. But Carey found it enjoyable to have so many things to focus on as well as being in a very wonderful routine again.

This morning was Matt's turn to cook them breakfast and he had decided on waffles with strawberry jam for her. She loved the waffles when he made them and she remembered during the Tip-to-Tip she ran through vast kilometers of strawberries, just enjoying the incredible smell.

So his waffles with strawberry jam really were a wonderful treat.

He was in the kitchen sort of humming to himself as he cooked and she was sitting at the kitchen table studying reports on the progress of the new, faster drives for the ships.

The new drives were now going to push the ships factors faster than even the Ancient drives could do. *Arcadia Case*, the Ancient's ship they had found first, had said it could get from the edge galaxy of the sphere to the Center in three hours using what it referred to as trans-tunnel thirty.

Star Fall's top speed was trans-tunnel twelve at the moment. All of the ships on board were also capable of doing that speed.

Trans-tunnel drive was basically opening a hole in space to allow ships to travel faster than light through the tunnel. The breakthrough of higher speeds had come when some scientists had figured out that you could open another trans-tunnel inside the first one, getting factors more speed.

Trans-tunnel twelve meant that *Star Fall* at that speed was moving through twelve open trans-tunnels, one inside the other. Trans-tunnel thirty meant the ship was moving through thirty open tunnels at the same time, one inside the other.

Star Fall had taken over fifty years, exploring all the way, to get from the Milky Way Galaxy to the Center at half speed, or basically trans-tunnel six. Trans-tunnel thirty would allow *Star Fall* to return to the Milky Way in just under a month.

The engineers from both the Seeders and the Ancients thought that forty was possible safely, meaning that *Star Fall* could return to the Milky Way Galaxy in just two days.

From the massive map that Cannard had given them of the locations of the other Seeders galaxies, it was going to take that kind of speed to get to them. *Star Fall* was still trying to update Seeders star maps with the extra information. The maps showed so much space far, far beyond the edge of anything the Seeders could see before.

After seeing that map, Carey was even happier they had all agreed to keep the military part of their exploration. No telling what was out there. And she was starting to think that the Ancients not having a military force was pretty damn stupid.

Sure, the universe seemed empty of life except for humans, Gray, and Cirrata.

But the universe also seemed to be an endless place full of endless possibilities.

Matt finally brought over the wonderful-smelling waffle and put it in front of her along with a small dish of strawberry jam. The jam almost smelled better than the waffle.

"I sure loved running two years ago through the strawberry farms," she said. "You can never get too much of that smell."

He laughed. "I had two kilometers in the onion fields. Trust me, you can get too much of that smell."

She spread the jam on her waffle and took a bite, enjoying the wonderful taste.

"Speaking of running," he said. "It's one month before the normal start date of the Tip-to-Tip. We going to postpone it again this year?"

She looked up at him sort of surprised. "Wow, that was a fast year."

"It was, wasn't it?" he said, smiling as he sat down with his waffle. He put peanut butter on his waffles with maple syrup. She had tried it once and decided to stick with her strawberry jam.

Writing Advice
from Dean Wesley Smith

"I don't see any pressing reason to postpone it again, do you?"

"Nope," he said. "And I think we should open it up to teams from *Star Mist* and *Star Rain*."

"And all the scientists who are here," Carey said, starting to feel excited about the race once again. "And even the Ancients can field teams if they want."

"It's going to make it the biggest race yet," Matt said. "But I think the course can handle it."

"We can set up The Tip Lounge with levels going back from the center course, all covered in tables and chairs for the duration of the start and end of the race," Carey said. "So people from all over the entire lounge can see the runners as they leave and enter. That way the place can seat thousands, all drinking and partying."

"That could be really fun," Matt said, laughing.

Carey dug back into her waffle, feeling more and more excited the more she thought about it.

"Privacy screen down," Matt said. "*Star Fall,* if we had over two thousand teams in a Tip-to-Tip race, all starting at ten minute intervals, how long would it take for every team to start?"

"Just under fourteen days," Star Fall said.

"Ouch, going to need to cut that down," Carey said, laughing.

"It would only take seven days for every team to start at five-minute intervals," Matt said. "That's possible."

"Very possible," Carey said, smiling at the love of her life. "So we going to do this?"

"Oh, heavens, yes," Matt said. "And that means this afternoon I got to get to the track. You up for joining me?"

"I am," Carey said, as she finished off the last of her waffle and pushed her plate forward. "And that's why I am not going to ask for a second wonderful waffle."

"Oh, oh," Matt said, smiling at her. "It's getting serious."

"It is," she said. "Got to go call the race committee and get them going on this. You better call your team, see if they have all recovered from their injuries from two years ago."

Matt laughed.

Carey was impressed that he didn't remind her that he had won last time. But she had a hunch she would hear enough of that over the next month.

And she was right.

SECTION NINE
The Race

FORTY-ONE

MATT WAS STUNNED at how fast the month went from when they decided to once again do the Tip-to-Tip relay to the start of the race. Now he and Carey were in their apartment getting ready to jump to The Tip to start their teams on the race. And both of them were so excited they could hardly talk.

During that month the Seeders and the Ancient scientists working on the drive speeds had actually managed to jump the top speed to trans-tunnel forty-two. And they all swore it would be safe, but they were going to try it on some drone ships in about a month to make sure.

And even better news, the refitting of the existing ships drives would be minor. Very minor, actually. And also a lot quicker.

So if the tests worked, in three months or so, they could start refitting and within one short year all Seeder ships here in the Sphere would be faster.

A week ago they had sent out the call to all the other Starburst ships to turn around and head for the Milky Way galaxy at top speeds. But if the conversion to the new faster speeds was as easy as the scientists were saying, teams of engineers could go through the breadcrumb trails left by all the Starburst ships and upgrade them to get them back faster.

Just as in the war, the Seeder technology was taking a giant jump forward.

So far the six chairmen had not mentioned to any of the Ancients the plan for their old home. Until a century or two had passed and all the science was even between the two cultures, the chairmen could see no reason to. Their focus now was to find out what was happening with all the other seeded groups of Seeders.

And that was unofficially the next mission for all the Starburst ships once all the upgrades were done. Only the six chairmen knew it at the moment, since the time wasn't right just yet to mention that either.

He and Carey had actually underestimated how many teams would be foolish enough to sign up from the other two Starburst ships. And there were even twenty teams full of Ancients from Command running the relay.

As Cannard said to Matt when he made a comment about that, "We may have lived a long time, doesn't mean we can't still exercise."

So the total number of ten-person teams starting the nine-thousand kilometer relay was two-thousand, six-hundred and five. And even though none of the other four chairmen were running, they all had an unofficial bet as to which ship would have the most finishing teams.

Matt had no doubt *Star Fall's* teams would win that easily because they had the most teams starting at eight hundred and nine. Besides, *Star Fall* teams had been doing this crazy race for twenty years. But he had a hunch that in a year the other two ships would put forward enough teams to give them a challenge.

Matt moved over to where Carey had just stood from tying her shoes. "Ready to go?"

"Excited and nervous, just like every year," she said.

He took her hand and they jumped to an open spot near the starting line.

The sounds of a thousand people all talking and laughing at the same time smashed into them. Matt couldn't believe the noise level.

And the feeling of excitement.

It seemed that after a year of stress and worry, this was exactly what a lot of people needed.

The other nine of her team were there, all excited as well. His team was all gathered nearby, also smiling and laughing.

And sitting off at a table near the starting line were Benny and Gina and Angie and Gage and Ray and Tacita and Cannard and Marie.

They were all drinking wine and clearly having a great time in the fantastic party atmosphere of The Tip.

Since they had another five minutes before she started, Matt took Carey's hand and they walked over to the table of other chairmen.

"We had to see this craziness for ourselves," Cannard said, almost yelling to make himself heard.

"Never seen a party like this before," Marie shouted, her smile filling her face from ear-to-ear.

"It goes on like this for days at the start," Carey shouted to them, "and then when teams start finishing it gets even crazier."

"Well, good luck you two," Benny said, raising his glass of wine.

"Have fun!" Angie shouted.

Matt and Carey waved and went back to their teams.

"Seems the kids know how to have some fun," Matt said into Carey's ear.

Carey kissed him and then said, "Just don't have too much fun. You know how I can gloat if my team beats yours."

"Not happening," he said, smiling.

And with that she went over and put on her tracking armband and moved to the starting line.

A moment later a large horn sounded and the light on her band turned green and she started off through the lounge, waving at the applauding chairmen and everyone else as she went.

Matt stood, cheering and watching her go, his voice drowned out in the massive cheers from the huge room.

A few moments later she vanished out of the door and into the wide hallway beyond.

He glanced around, trying to take it all in. No matter how much the responsibility, the dangers they all faced, they had to remember that having fun was an important element to living.

And it couldn't get any more fun than this.

He turned back to his team who all cheered as he put on his tracking band.

Then he stepped to the starting line and to massive cheers that seemed to shake the entire room, the horn sounded, his light turned green and he started off running, saluting the other chairmen as he went past.

It was a long race, but he had a hunch that again this year he and his team would finish it.

Just like he and Carey and the other chairmen finished anything they started, no matter how long it took.

It was just who they were.

~

Can't Get Enough of Poker Boy?
These stories and more are available at your favorite booksellers.

Coming Next Issue in *Smith's Monthly*

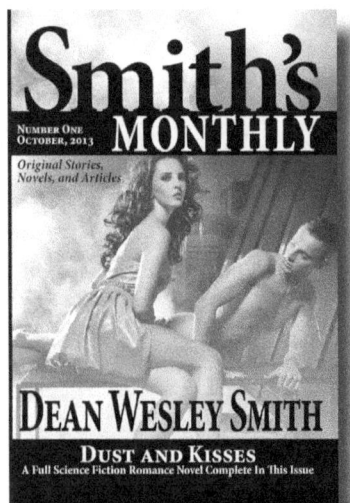

#1...October 2013

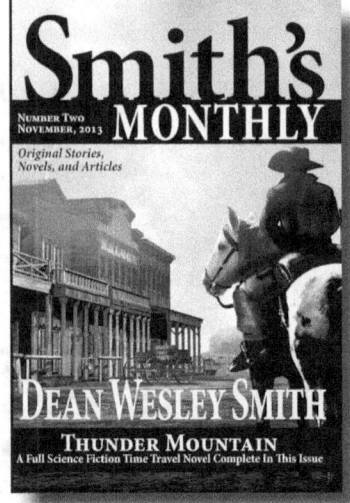

#2...November 2013

#3...December 2013

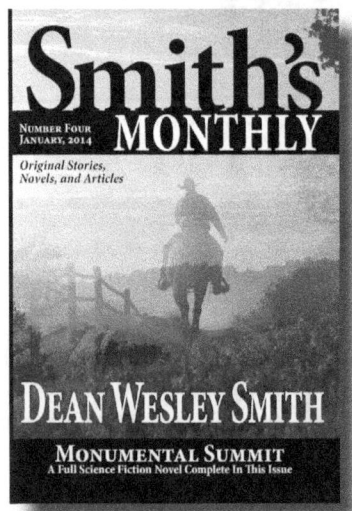

#4...January 2014

#5...February 2014

#6...March 2014

#7...April 2014

#8...May 2014

#9...June 2014

#10...July 2014

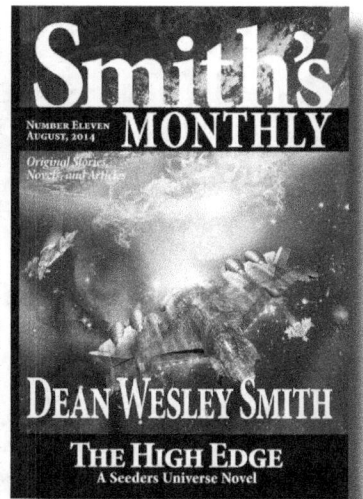

#11...August 2014

#12...September 2014

#13...October 2014

#14...November 2014

#15...December 2014

#16...January 2015

#17...February 2015

#18...March 2015

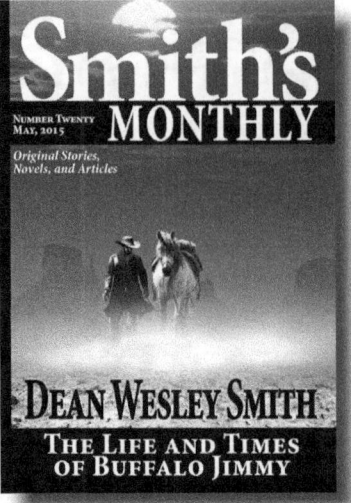

#19...April 2015 *#20...May 2015* *#21...June 2015*

#22...July 2015 *#23...August 2015* *#24...September 2015*

#25...October 2015 *#26...November 2015* *#27...December 2015*

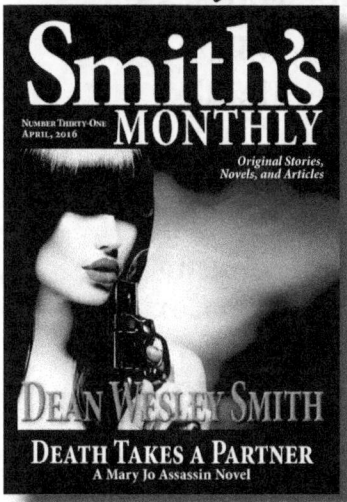

Thank You!!

I would like to thank the following wonderful people who support my blog and my work through Patreon. Your support is very important to me. Thanks!

Betsy Wilcox
Irette Y. Patterson
Kathryn Rooney
Wendy Lee Maddox
Jamie Curierre
Chris Cousino
Jane Lawson
Shantnu Tiwari
Miguel Angel Alonso Pulido
Nancy Hendrickson
Ryan M. Williams
Jacob Proffitt
Marian Goldeen
Gary Speer
Megan Bryce
Michelle Tatam
Ann Tucker
Kari Wolfe
Albert Lemke
Stacey Larson
Diane Darcy
Krystle Jones
Kari Gallagher
T. Thorn Coyle
Tasha Turner Lennhoff

Erick Lindman
Christopher Ridge
Terry Mixon
James Husun
Sherman Cox
Chong Go
Maria Grace
Grondpom
Fen
Robin Brande
J.R. Murdock
Kathleen McClure
Gunnar Gunderson
F.I. Goldhaber
Mary Jo Rabe
John Kilgallon
Dave Hendrickson
Jabberwocky
Eric Goebelbecker
Marsha Kessler
Scott Gordon
Martyn Folkes
John
Cj Lehi
Brenda Smith